THE WITNESS

Maggie Black Case Files #2

JACK MCSPORRAN

inked entertainment

Series Guide

The main Maggie Black Series consists of full-length novels featuring secret agent Maggie Black.

The Maggie Black Case Files is a prequel series of self-contained missions which Maggie completed prior to the events of the main Maggie Black Series.

Both series can be read before, after, or in conjunction with the other.

Maggie Black Case Files

Book 1: Vendetta
Book 2: The Witness
Book 3: The Defector

Maggie Black Series

Book 1: Kill Order
Book 2: Hit List (Coming Spring 2018)

For my dear friend, Sam.

Chapter 1

Maggie Black leapt from the edge of the rooftop and flew through the air.

Below, boats passed through the canal, carting tourists around the crowded city as they snapped pictures with excited fingers.

Pain shot up Maggie's feet and traveled through her tired legs as she landed hard on top of the next building, muscles twitching in complaint. Maggie grit her teeth and continued her chase. The killer couldn't get away.

Quickening her pace, Maggie jumped the gap. But instead of reaching the next rooftop, the buildings faded into shadows, and she found herself plunged into the ice-cold water of the lagoon. Rope bound her to a wooden post in the darkness. The tide was rising, inching closer and closer to her face, ready to devour her.

And Leon.

"I love you, Maggie."

From the murky, bone-chilling water, to the hot jets of a double shower, Maggie leaned into Leon as he kissed her neck. The rush of their near-death experience set fire to the simmering passion that had rekindled at the start of their mission in Venice.

Steam rose around them and washed away the image, reforming in the bed where they spent hours beneath the sheets, lost in the complete ecstasy of their insatiable need for each other.

Faces flashed in Maggie's mind. Two dead crime bosses. One with a bullet through his throat, the other stabbed in the back. A dead undercover agent shot point blank after being discovered. A British drug dealer. And Angela Rossi, the woman behind it all.

The roar of an engine filled her ears. Wind whipped across Maggie's hair.

"Closer," she urged Leon, holding a detonator in her hand.

The speedboat rushed through the lagoon, the waves tossing the boat up and down as they crashed through the water, leaving a track of white foam in their wake.

Maggie pressed the button on the device, and the boat they were chasing—Angela's boat—exploded.

A blast of heat rushed over her face, and Maggie startled in her bed.

She blinked and cataloged the scene around her. The sun crawled over familiar walls, and she turned to find a bedside table—*her* bedside table—with an alarm clock announcing it was just after six in the morning. She was home. In her flat in London.

A wave of nausea coursed through her from the boat chase, making her head spin.

No, not the boat chase. That was two months ago now.

The nausea was something else.

Maggie stumbled to the bathroom, disorientated from her dream, and dropped to her knees by the toilet. Her body convulsed, and she heaved, reaching the bowl with not a moment to spare. Maggie lost track of time as she hugged the cool porcelain and her stomach emptied itself for the third morning in a row.

Sweat beaded her forehead, and she leaned against the corner of the bathtub, wiping her mouth with the back of her hand. She closed her eyes until her head stopped spinning, letting the feeling pass before she tried to get up.

On shaking legs, Maggie leaned over the sink and ran the cold water. She splashed it over her face and neck, avoiding the mirror. Her blond hair hung in a curtain over her face, tousled from another restless night of troubled dreams.

Maggie dabbed her face dry with a towel and flushed the toilet, plopping down on the closed lid. Her eyes drifted over to the plastic bag sitting by her toiletries. She'd purchased the item a few days ago, but she hadn't quite mustered the courage to use it.

A tremor shook her hands, and Maggie tucked them into her folded arms. She wouldn't show fear. Not even to herself. Still, she worried at her lip as she debated her next move.

Eight weeks had passed since her mission in Venice. It felt longer than that in some ways, each day without Leon stretching longer than the last. Yet the nightmares kept the horror of the trip fresh in her mind like it had happened only yesterday.

With their mission complete, she and Leon had spent the rest of the week in the sinking city like a pair of newly-weds. They saw little of the city besides their shared hotel room, barely coming up for air as they enjoyed their temporary reprieve from their lives as secret agents.

Maggie's heart panged at the thought of him. Of his infectious smile and comforting presence. The way he looked at her with his dark, honest eyes. She missed his touch, missed the way he'd found all the places that made her moan.

She gave herself a shake.

Leon was off on a new assignment, disappeared to some undisclosed location doing something classified for the good of Queen and country.

Maggie had only just gotten back from a quick job in Dublin herself. She'd been tasked with taking out an IRA radical before he could meet up with a militia group in the Middle East. The job went smoothly, even with the queasiness that had followed her around like a stalker on the prowl, ready and waiting for her every morning without fail.

She stole another glance at the bag, a pit of dread forming in her stomach. She couldn't put it off forever. Maggie sighed and reached for the bag, pulling out the box within, and reading the instructions on the back. It was a straightforward process.

Maggie opened the box and looked inside, her fingers trembling. She closed the box.

It could wait another day.

Another day of wondering, of biting her fingernails and thinking about nothing else. Another day of not knowing.

Before she could change her mind, Maggie removed the little plastic stick and considered the terrifying apparatus. How could something so small have the power to turn a trained secret agent into such a nervous wreck? The weight of what it might reveal turned her already queasy stomach.

Maggie removed the cap and proceeded with the unglamorous process. Soon, she'd know the answer to the question she couldn't even vocalize. The question she couldn't even bring herself to admit to Ashton, her best friend, and trusted confidant. She'd visited him the day before and hadn't said a word.

Now all she had to do was wait. Maggie replaced the cap and placed the test down by the sink. She studied the offending piece of plastic and paced the small bathroom.

Her palms grew clammy.

She hadn't paid much attention to the lull in her usual cycle, chalking it up to the stress of the job. Her body never ran a normal monthly routine anyway, not even back when she was a teenager.

In the months before Venice, Maggie had neglected her prescribed little white pill. Her social life was non-existent thanks to her work. Hopping from one place to the next without a word to anyone didn't exactly do wonders for a girl's love life. Not that she'd had any recent interest in one.

At least, not until she saw Leon again.

Maggie padded on bare feet into her bedroom and checked the time.

Three minutes felt like three hours.

A buzzing vibrated by her bed. Maggie flinched, reaching on reflex for the gun she kept under her pillow, but it was only her phone.

She sighed and placed a hand on her chest as she collected her phone, heart drumming with anticipation and dread.

"Bishop." Her boss was the only one who'd call that early.

"Morning, Maggie. I hope I haven't woke you."

Maggie ran a hand through her hair. "No, I was up." She glanced over her shoulder to the bathroom. "What's going on?"

Bishop sipped on something at his end, a morning cup of tea no doubt. "We have a situation. I need you to come in as soon as possible."

A jolt of panic coursed through her. "What's wrong? Is it Leon?"

"What?" Bishop asked, surprise coloring his tone. "No, no, he's fine. I need you on a new assignment. I'll tell you more when you come in."

Maggie's shoulders dropped, and she pinched the bridge of her nose, trying to calm herself down. "Okay, give me an hour."

"See you then." Bishop hung up without waiting for a goodbye.

The room grew silent again, and Maggie noted the time.

Her three minutes were up.

She returned to the bathroom on hesitant feet and readied herself for the result. Maggie peered down at the little plastic stick. Two blue lines stared up at her.

She was pregnant.

Chapter 2

Maggie reached the Unit headquarters in a blur, too lost in her troubled thoughts to take notice of how she got there.

She swiped her security pass at the doors of the five-story office building—which masked as a stationery supplier named Inked International—and continued past the foyer in a daze, not saying hello to anyone. The elevators dinged at her boss's floor before Maggie even registered she'd left the lobby.

Like always, Brice Bishop waited for her in the hallway when the doors pinged opened.

"Maggie," he said, placing a paternal hand on her back and leading her into his office. "Thank you for coming in."

"No problem." Maggie kept her leather jacket on, unable to scare away the chill that enveloped her. It was cold outside, and any residual heat from the two weeks of sunshine Londoners called summer had left weeks ago.

Bishop held up a teapot adorned with the British flag, steam trailing from the spout. "Tea?"

"Yes, please," Maggie said, taking a seat at the conference table.

Bishop wore a navy suit, the tailoring impeccable on his frame. For a man in his late fifties, he was in great shape. Despite trading in fieldwork for his desk job years ago, the Unit Chief hadn't lost his edge. Even his chestnut hair was kept army regulation short from his days in the military.

After fixing her tea with milk and no sugar, Bishop sat across from her and slid the mug over the table.

Maggie cupped the warm ceramic and let the heat seep into her hands.

"Is everything all right?" Bishop paused with his mug hovering by his lips as he took her in, a little crease forming above his brow.

"Just tired, that's all," she lied, fixing her face into a smile. She should have known Bishop would sense the change in her mood; he knew her too well by now. After working together for eleven years—four in training and seven with Maggie as an official agent—they'd cemented an intimate knowledge of each other's emotions. They were abundantly familiar with the other's subtle ticks and tells. Maggie took a soothing sip of tea and hid her racing mind behind a cool façade.

Bishop studied her for a moment with his piercing brown eyes before getting back to business. "You can get some sleep on the plane."

"Where am I going?"

"New York City."

It had been a long time since she was in the United States. Americans took great pride in their covert intelligence work and rarely sought British assistance unless the situation impacted both nations.

Maggie sipped her tea, an English breakfast blend that soothed her stomach enough that she craved a solid meal. She placed her hand over her belly and fought the swell of emotion that grew inside her.

"What's the situation?" she asked, shaking her emotions aside. She couldn't give Bishop more room to draw suspicions.

Bishop gave a little laugh, though Maggie didn't miss the thinning of his lips. "I'm not quite sure, actually."

Maggie frowned. "What?"

"It's all very hush, hush." Bishop shrugged and laced his fingers together. "The Director left orders to send you across the pond for the official briefing."

For a moment, Maggie just sat there, blinking. She couldn't recall a time when Bishop wasn't briefed on an assignment. He oversaw every agent in the Unit, which meant he knew about all the missions Director-General Helmsley and the other higher-ups delegated to their intelligence agency. Given the covert nature of their work, sometimes agents weren't cleared to discuss their jobs with their colleagues. But Bishop always knew. At least, he was supposed to.

Maggie sat up in her chair, tea abandoned. "Why haven't you been briefed?"

"It's above my pay grade, it seems."

Part of her rigorous training involved reading people, a vital skill in the field, one that made sure you returned alive. But Maggie didn't need a degree in behavioral psychology to see how much Bishop bristled at not being privy to the job at hand.

"What *do* you know?" Bishop must know something. If only enough to choose the best agent for such a highly-classified mission.

Bishop leaned back in his chair and shook his head. "Only that it concerns a key witness to something important, and that the mission is of the highest priority. Apparently, our national security is in jeopardy, and the Director wants my best agent on it as soon as possible."

Even after eleven years, Bishop's praise still invoked a sense of pride in Maggie. She'd worked hard during her time as an agent, never turning down an assignment or giving up and coming home when things got rough.

But could she accept the mission now?

Taking a prolonged drink of her tea, she considered her options. She had no idea what she was going to do about being pregnant. Having a child was never part of her plan. Never something she allowed herself to think about for too long, given her occupation.

There was so much to consider, and Maggie wasn't ready for any of it. There'd be time for that later.

"When do I leave?" she asked. Whatever was happening in America was clearly urgent. If her skill set were needed, then she would give all the help she could, just as she had always done. The rest could wait until she returned home.

"A car is waiting outside to take you to the airport."

Maggie pushed her chair back and stood. "I'll need to stop at my apartment for a few things first."

"Already taken care of," said Bishop with an apologetic smile. "Someone will be waiting at the airport with your things."

"Well," Maggie said, prickling at the idea of someone breaking into her apartment and rummaging through her belongings. "I guess I'm all set to go then."

Bishop walked her to the door. "Once you land, you'll report to the British Consulate."

Maggie shot him a raised eyebrow. "This is all very cloak and dagger. Even by our standards."

"Agreed," said Bishop, a little weary now. It wasn't even eight o'clock yet, and Maggie would bet the man had been at the office for hours already. If he even went home the night before.

"Thanks for the tea." Maggie placed a hand on his

shoulder before turning to leave. "I'll see you when I get back."

"Ring me if you need anything," Bishop called as she stepped into the elevator to take her down to the awaiting car. "Oh, and Maggie?"

"Yes?" she asked, as the cart doors began to close.

Bishop's face hardened, his eyes troubled. "Watch your back on this one."

Maggie nodded. "I always do."

Chapter 3

NEW YORK CITY, UNITED STATES OF AMERICA

Maggie left London from Heathrow at eleven in the morning and touched down at JFK International Airport a little after two in the afternoon, thanks to the five-hour difference between time zones.

Despite the routine of hopping on a plane at a moment's notice and flying across the world being as normal for Maggie as taking the tube to work, even she couldn't avoid jet lag altogether. Over the years, she'd grown accustomed to the lethargic sluggishness that accompanied her travels.

As tired as she was, catching some sleep on the way to

the consulate was out of the question. Her mind hadn't stopped spinning since the test came out positive. Talk about a wakeup call.

Wheeling the carry-on suitcase one of her fellow agents had packed for her, Maggie made her way through security, putting on an air of excited tourist for customs. A driver stood outside the arrivals terminal carrying a little whiteboard with her name scrawled on it.

"Ms. Black?" he asked, no doubt having been provided a picture of her beforehand.

"The very one." Maggie handed him her luggage and followed him to his car. She swung open the Escalade's passenger door and slipped inside. The Cadillac stood out like fox in a hen house among the rows of yellow cabs, with its V8 engine and tinted windows. Apparently, subtlety wasn't a concern.

After stowing her case in the trunk, the driver settled behind the wheel and pulled into traffic. "I'm to take you straight to the consulate."

Maggie suppressed rolling her eyes. It wasn't the driver's fault, but the babysitting was a little ridiculous. She'd been sent in response to a request for the Unit's best operative; her US-based colleagues should trust her to make it from the airport to the consulate without getting herself killed.

Situated in Manhattan, the British Consulate General resided in the Turtle Bay neighborhood of Midtown East. The trip from the airport should have taken thirty minutes, but thanks to traffic, an hour passed and they were still on the road.

The driver slowed to a stop to pay the toll, and they crossed the East River through the Queens-Midtown Tunnel. The Empire State Building poked out from the skyline beyond, waving at them before the view vanished and was replaced with the mouth of the tunnel.

Phosphorescent lights glowed above them and guided the way through the underwater highway before it finally opened out into Manhattan. Taking the Downtown exit, they merged onto East 37th Street and turned right onto 3rd Avenue.

Maggie craned her neck to get a view of the towering buildings looming over them from every direction, their postures dominant and proud. There was something about the city that always made Maggie pause. She'd traveled the world twice over working for the Unit, spent time on every continent and experienced the cities each had to offer.

New York didn't have the gilded statues and ornate facades of Paris, or the ethereal decaying beauty of Venice. It didn't have the tranquility of Kyoto or the deep-rooted history of Edinburgh with its castle perched on top of an ancient volcano.

Yet it had *something*.

A presence that could be felt more than seen. A confident energy that lived and breathed through the gridded streets and skyscrapers. A resilience in the people who stomped the sidewalks, from hard-nosed construction workers to high-end businesswomen in expensive heels. In both the old-timers who watched the city grow and polish itself over decades and the new arrivals fresh off the bus with big dreams and a determined grit to succeed.

It was heard in the voices of performers in Harlem's Apollo Theater. Tasted in the dirty water hotdogs from the cart vendors around Times Square. Witnessed in the cut-throat world of the stock market on Wall Street. Experienced through the actors on the legendary stages of Broadway.

The city held no pretenses, and living there wasn't for the faint-hearted. The old adage held true: you could make it anywhere if you could handle the Big Apple. It was the very thing that made the place special.

It attracted tourists from every corner of the globe, each of them eager to experience that special, intangible *something*, if only for a day.

New York City was unlike any other place in the world.

The car pulled up at 845 3rd Avenue, and Maggie stepped out into the street. The front entrance of the large, modern office building greeted her with a British flag swaying from a pole on one side and the American stars and stripes hanging at the other.

The driver led Maggie inside, greeting the guards who manned the doors. The pair of guards ushered Maggie through a metal detector and passed her luggage across the conveyor belt of an x-ray machine before allowing her entry. Once satisfied she wasn't carrying a bomb or packing a gun, they formally welcomed Maggie to the consulate.

To the untrained eye, the foyer appeared pedestrian. Clusters of people sat around as they waited for their appointments and filled in forms. A loud and exasperated man at the front desk explained how he'd lost his passport.

Maggie spotted the cameras positioned throughout, some prominently displayed to deter misbehavior, others hidden and focused on strategic points. While consulates acted as safe havens for nationals, they were also potential targets, and the New York location wasn't taking any chances.

Security may appear lax on the surface, but a trained—and heavily armed—detail of marines or private contractors was undoubtedly standing by, ready to act if the need arose.

A woman spotted Maggie and approached.

"Maggie Black," she said, holding out her hand. "I'm Danielle Hawkins."

Like her demeanor, Danielle's shake was firm and professional. She nodded to the driver, who took that as a sign to leave, having passed his charge onto someone else.

"I appreciate the escort, but I could have made it here myself." Maggie's gaze trailed after the driver as he left, noting the way he paused to speak with the security guards at the x-ray machine.

"Just giving you a warm welcome," Danielle replied, herding her over to the elevators.

More like keeping an eye on her.

No older than thirty, Danielle kept her mouse-brown hair pulled back from her face, the spray of freckles across her nose giving her a juvenile appearance. Even the thick mascara and tight-fitting suit couldn't hide her youth.

Six stories up, Maggie trailed her case behind her as she walked through a busy cubicle-filled floor decorated with an art installation of the British flag running along one of the walls.

"I apologize for the lack of a proper welcome, but I'm afraid time is of the essence." Danielle led her into a small room in the back where two other suits waited for them.

Danielle shut the door behind her and closed the blinds of the glass office.

"Ms. Black." The eldest of the two men flashed a tight smile from his position at the top of a mahogany conference table.

"Maggie, this is the Consul-General, Jonathan Cole."

No one bothered to introduce the man at Cole's left, leading Maggie to conclude he was the Consul-General's secretary or personal assistant. Hierarchy was king in places like the consulate, and Cole wouldn't even think to introduce someone with such a low position.

Danielle sat to Jonathan's right, leaving Maggie to sit at the opposite end of the table like she was a schoolgirl sent to the headmaster's office. A deliberate move on their part, she was sure. Not that it intimidated her in the slightest.

"I understand the situation is time sensitive," Maggie said, uninterested in introductions. The Unit sent her there for a reason, and it was about time she learned why.

"Indeed." Jonathan's assistant slid over a document, which the Consul-General scanned through rimless glasses. "Which department did you say you came from?"

"I didn't."

At that, Jonathan Cole leaned back in his chair and folded his arms across his ample gut, the buttons of his shirt struggling against the pressure.

"Look." Maggie breathed deep and grasped at the final straws of her patience. "I'm here because the higher-ups feel you need my help. Clearly, you aren't happy with an outsider joining whatever operation you have going on. I can't say I'm particularly thrilled, either, but given how tight-lipped everyone is about the situation, I assume something major has happened. So why don't we stop this little power play before it starts, and you tell me what I need to know."

Silence fell over the room, full of barely contained tension. Finally, Danielle cleared her throat and looked to Jonathan, who nodded his permission.

"The sole witness to the murder of a UN official has been abducted." Danielle let out a resigned sigh. "We need someone to get her back."

"Which is where I come in, I presume." Maggie knew

a thing or two about recovering hostages. "Where is she being held?"

"The Russian Consulate."

Maggie's eyebrows shot up. "Excuse me?"

Danielle fidgeted in her chair. "The Russians got to the witness before we could and are holding her inside. Our sources say they plan to move her tomorrow afternoon."

"So you expect me to infiltrate the consulate and do what exactly? Stage a breakout?"

"We were told the higher-ups were sending their best agent." Jonathan glanced up from his file like it was nothing. Like accomplishing what they asked was as simple as a walk in Central Park. As if Maggie could just waltz up to the Russians and ask if they would be so kind as to go fetch the witness and hand her over.

"Who's the witness?" Maggie asked.

"Her name is Emily Wallace." Danielle passed over a photo, and the face of a young black girl smiled up at her. She was dressed in a school uniform, had braces covering her white teeth, and wore her hair in long braids that fell past her shoulders.

"She's just a kid." Maggie held out an expectant hand for the rest on the intel, and the three of them blinked back at her. "There's no file?"

Jonathan seemed to roll his words over in his mind before responding. "Due to the nature of the situation, we're not at liberty to disclose more about the witness."

"Fine. Who was the UN official?"

Again, neither of them seemed inclined to answer.

"You're not going to tell me that either?" Maggie shook her head and laughed. "I get it. The less I know, the less the Russians can torture out of me if I get caught trying to save Emily Wallace."

"If you are caught, the British government will not claim you as their own," Jonathan warned.

Maggie knew the drill. The chances of her succeeding in the monumental task laid before her were slim. Slim enough for them not to tell her anything other than the bare minimum.

"When did the Russian's kill the official?" Whomever, the victim, was, they must have been British. Otherwise, this impossible task would have fallen to someone else. Additional details about their identity would be useful but, ultimately, unnecessary.

"The incident happened last night," said the Consul-General. "The American's are doing what they can to stop the news reaching the press."

"Emily Wallace is the only person who saw the assassination," Danielle added. "Given the method used, there is nothing else to prove the death wasn't due to natural causes."

Maggie nodded. Without Emily, the Russians would get away with it. Emily was the only link to prove their guilt, and Maggie's government would need her testimony.

Jonathan sat up straight, his defensive guard replaced

with grave authority. "It is vital the witness make it back here alive. Failure to do so could result in the highest threat to national security in years."

No pressure then.

Maggie frowned. "Why haven't they killed her already?"

"The Americans are pursuing official channels to enter the Russian Consulate." Jonathan removed his glasses, exposing dark circles under his eyes. "We think the Russians don't want to risk killing Ms. Wallace inside the building as it could incriminate them. Especially with the US watching from outside. Better to slip her out unnoticed, take her somewhere unrelated, and kill her there."

Most civilians assumed consulates and embassies were built on foreign soil. Maggie blamed the movies. While the diplomats and ambassadors benefited from diplomatic immunity, the Russian Consulate was on sovereign territory belonging to the US.

The trouble came from entering the building itself. Strictly speaking, American authorities required the Consulate's permission to come inside. Barging in without the Russian Consul-General's consent would create a political nightmare and cause serious repercussions to foreign relations.

The Russians wouldn't be quick to open their doors with Emily Wallace inside. By the time the Americans got in, the witness would be long gone. Which meant Maggie was the only person who could save Emily and help prove that the Russians were responsible for the UN official's murder.

Maggie hesitated in her chair, hand hovering over the picture of Emily Wallace.

The Russian Consulate was a fortress. This was more than a simple case of breaking and entering to reach the witness. Assuming she even got that far. The Russians would be on high alert and were already planning on killing one person. They wouldn't think twice about adding Maggie to the list if they caught her.

Could she risk it?

Normally, Maggie wouldn't think twice. She'd sworn long ago to give her life for the good of her country. But if she failed now, it wouldn't just be her life forfeited. She had more than herself to consider.

Maggie picked up the photo and stared at the girl's innocent face. Emily was someone's child. Someone's baby. Maggie couldn't even begin to imagine what her parents must be going through. Their daughter stolen with no way to get her back. Standing helpless by the phone and unable to do anything.

Maggie wasn't helpless. *She* could do something.

She could get up and leave. Return home and forget all about it. It would be the smart thing to do. She ran an absent hand over her stomach and averted her eyes from the photo.

If she walked away now, Emily would be just as dead

as the UN official, and no one would be brought to justice for either of them.

Maggie caught Emily's kind eyes from the photo and sighed. Sometimes the right thing to do wasn't always the smart thing.

"Well, you've all been a wonderful help," she said, her words dripping with sarcasm. "Do I at least get a weapon, or is that too much to ask?"

Jonathan's assistant handed Maggie a rucksack.

She dug inside and brought out a 9mm Glock 19, extra magazines and rounds, and a foreign passport with her picture inside. Just another day at the office.

"You'll find a full biography in there as well," said Danielle. "I hear aliases are your specialty."

Maggie closed the Russian passport. "You heard right."

Chapter 4

The thirty-five-story condominium was just as Maggie expected: a lavish residence in the Upper West Side complete with a host of amenities, including its own swimming pool, basketball court, yoga studio, and sauna.

The glass tower on West 59th Street resided in the heart of Lincoln Square, and Maggie unlocked the door to the apartment on the twenty-eighth floor.

Maggie let out a whistle as she took in her temporary digs, dumping her suitcase in the corner along with her new backpack and the supplies she collected on the way there. Ashton had called ahead with orders for the doorman to hand over the spare key when she arrived, her best friend refusing to let her stay in a hotel while she was in New York.

"It's not like I'm using the place," he'd said on the phone that morning before she left.

Ashton had several homes scattered around the world, all of them owned but none through legitimate means. Maggie may carry out illegal acts for the government, but Ashton preferred to do his nefarious business on his own terms, having left the Unit years ago without ever looking back.

He'd done well for himself since then. Most of Ashton's fortune came from ripping off criminals who had no idea he'd duped them. Maggie wandered around the two-bedroom apartment, everything furnished like a showroom—from the four-poster bed in the master suite, to the plush suede couches in the living-room which led out into a wide corner terrace—and took in the view of the Hudson River.

Maggie stepped outside and let the cool breeze sweep over her face. It had been a long day, and tomorrow was fast approaching.

When the sun dipped low, and the air drew goosebumps along her arms, Maggie returned inside and ran a hot bath, filling it high with bubbles. Steam rose from the water as she sank beneath the sudsy surface and let the heat seep in and loosen her tense muscles.

She closed her eyes and basked in the quiet.

The peaceful silence broke when her phone buzzed against the tiled floor. Maggie groaned and reached over the edge of the bath to put the caller on loudspeaker.

"Hello?"

"Mags, how you doing?" Ashton's Scottish brogue reverberated around the bathroom.

Her fingers brushed over her flat stomach, and she stared down, the image of it swollen with her growing baby sweeping through her mind.

"Good," Maggie lied, giving herself a shake and pushing the image to the back of her mind. She sat up and folded her arms on the tub's ledge, leaning towards the phone and wishing Ashton was with her.

"You settled in okay?"

"The apartment's a little shabby, but I guess it'll do," she teased, making a better effort to hide her troubled mind with Ashton than she had with Bishop.

"Brilliant," Ashton said. A woman's voice spoke in the background, announcing several delays to upcoming flights.

Maggie frowned. "Where are you?"

"At a layover in Miami. I'm heading to Ecuador."

Maggie narrowed her eyes. "What are you doing down there?"

"You know me," Ashton said, all innocent. "A wee bit of this, a wee bit of that."

"Well, be careful. I'm tied up here, so I can't come and save your arse like I did in New Orleans." Ashton was no stranger to sticky situations, but that particular trip had been a close one. Too close.

Ashton laughed like the trip had consisted of gumbo,

good jazz music, and one too many cocktails, instead of murder and mayhem. "I'll be on my best behavior."

"That's not promising much," Maggie chided, but she couldn't stop the grin tugging at the corners of her lips, despite her growing worry.

"Is something wrong?"

Maggie sighed. "It's just work. Nothing to worry about."

"You sure?"

"Yes, I'm fine," she assured, changing the subject. "Thanks for letting me stay here."

"Of course." Another airport announcement sounded in the distance. "I better go, my flight is boarding."

"Stay safe."

"You, too," Ashton replied, before hanging up.

Maggie shook her head. If there were trouble to be found in Ecuador, Ashton would find it.

Strictly speaking, Maggie shouldn't have told Ashton she was in the city on assignment. Especially given the sensitive nature of the job. Old habits die hard though, and they had always kept in touch, checking in with each other even after Ashton left the Unit. Besides, the Unit wasn't aware they'd remained friends; the entire agency had been ordered to cut all ties with the 'traitor.' Not that Maggie listened. As long as they kept their friendship covert, everyone was happy.

Laying back into the water, she indulged in a further

ten minutes of attempted relaxation before drying off. It was time to get to work.

Maggie wrapped a towel around her and sat in front of the dressing table in the master bedroom. She propped the background document of her new alias by the mirror.

Yana Kostina.

As far as the look went, it wasn't that difficult. Maggie could keep her natural hair if she wanted since the fake passport was several years old. Yana's hair was a lighter shade than hers, but people changed their hairstyle all the time. In the end, she decided to match the picture exactly. With a mission this sensitive, she couldn't risk any slip-ups. Nothing to make the people inside the Russian Consulate pause or question her.

Tucking her real hair under a cap, Maggie put on the newly purchased wig she got from a little place in the East Village and pinned it in place. Teasing it out to give the hair more volume, she styled the platinum blond bob into a deliberate messy look to fit Yana's free-spirited personality.

Yana Kostina was born and raised in Cherepovets, the largest city in Vologda Oblast. The daughter of an architect and a notable oil painter, Yana grew to hold a deep appreciation and love for the arts. So much so, that it led her to study the subject at Saint Petersburg University where she earned a master's degree in art criticism.

"I work at a gallery in Cherepovets," Maggie said into the mirror. Yana returned home after she graduated and quickly became the associate art director for a thriving gallery known in the art world for its industrial inspired installations.

Yana's eyes were darker than Maggie's, a deeper, warmer shade than her ice blue irises. Nothing a set of contacts couldn't fix. Unscrewing the cap, Maggie slid the contacts over her eyes and blinked them into place.

"I've always wanted to visit New York," she said in Yana's native tongue.

Maggie repeated the phrase a few times, getting the accent just right. She had learned Russian from a Muscovite, and while the language was uniform across the country, there were subtle differences in tone and inflection. Yana's Northwestern roots should be apparent when she spoke, at least to fellow Russians at the consulate.

Playing a tourist was the ideal set up for Maggie's plan. She wasn't too concerned about infiltrating the Russian Consulate. Getting inside was one thing. It was getting back out that worried her.

Once they learned Emily Wallace had escaped their clutches, the Russians would stop at nothing to contain the situation, even if it meant killing Maggie and Emily on the streets.

Satisfied with Yana's appearance, Maggie rummaged in her shopping bags and brought out her outfit for tomorrow. She made sure to buy flats for the mission. The only thing worse than breakout missions were breakout missions in heels.

The boots she chose were black leather with steel

toecaps. While not conventional footwear for a tourist, they fit with Yana's quirky style and could also come in handy if she found herself in a fight. Maggie matched the boots with some tightfitting black jeans, red cardigan, and a tank top with a picture of a little cartoon cat on the front.

Maggie slipped into the clothes and took in her new persona through the full-length mirror by the bed. While not to Maggie's taste, Yana was exactly what she needed to be: young, unassuming, and innocent.

She was ready for tomorrow.

Chapter 5

M aggie walked up Madison Avenue and turned left onto East 91st Street.

A light wind picked up, the trees along the sidewalks ruffling in a choreographed dance to the whistling breeze. The Russian consulate stood in the middle of the street, a grand four-story building which seemed welcoming from the outside with its potted plants by the windows. Inside would be an entirely different story.

Like the British Consulate, its Russian counterpart would have a specialized team on guard, waiting to end any potential conflicts, with lethal force if necessary. Surveillance cameras were deliberately visible at each corner of the building, two trained on the front door with the Russian flag hanging proudly above it. Another camera watched from the gate adjacent to the building where cars had to wait until they were permitted entry.

Maggie stored the layout and camera positions in her mind for later. Exit routes were a priority, and if the Russians were as prepared as the British, they could lock the building down in mere minutes.

Stopping at the consulate's neighbors next door, Maggie ducked under the scaffolding erected over the outer building and put the finishing touches to her disguise. Construction workers called to each other, men on the roof tossing bricks and other debris into a chute which traveled down the scaffolding and straight into a large dumpster. Cosmetic work from the looks of it. The city had cleaned itself up over the years, and residents so close to the park had to keep up appearances. It wouldn't do to be the shabbiest building on the block.

Maggie kept a fresh face to give herself a younger appearance, the only make-up on her face there to give the illusion of an injury, a new and reddening mark that promised to grow into a nasty bruise.

She bit down on the capsule in her mouth. The contents burst open, filling her mouth with the tang of cinnamon. Maggie let the liquid spill over her bottom lip and drip down her chin, the fake blood stark red against her pale skin.

Speeding up her breathing, she took short, shallow breaths. Her heartbeat quickened and pulsed in her chest, her body reacting to the deliberate signs of physical distress. She paced a little, back and forth, running a hand through her hair. It wasn't enough to simply act. You had to *be*.

Maggie forced herself back to when she was a child, bringing up memories that brought out the worst of her panic response. The day her mother died. The night she killed her first man in self-defense. Of when she was arrested for said murder and held in a police station. Of when she and Leon almost drowned in Venice, just weeks ago.

It didn't take long for the emotions to overtake her logical mind. Maggie welcomed the rising panic and had to force back the urge to shut those memories away. They were painful, but they also had their uses. Her past could very well help ensure her future.

Tearing her cardigan and letting one of the sleeves hang over her shoulder, Maggie limped the rest of the way down the street and stumbled through the front doors of the consulate.

"Help!" she cried in Russian as soon as she entered. "Somebody, please, help me."

A startled guard stood beside the metal detectors.

Maggie ran past him and through the detectors before he could stop her, the siren wailing as she passed.

Another guard approached her from her left. Maggie spotted him in her periphery, but Yana wouldn't have, given the state she was in. Instead, she rushed forward, unaware of his approach and headed past the front foyer and down an empty hallway.

"Wait, you can't go back there." The man grabbed her arm and yanked her back, his vice grip wrapping the whole way around her upper arm.

Maggie restrained herself. Normally, she'd punch the guard in the throat for touching her. But Yana didn't have the training or instinct for violence. "Please, you must help me," Maggie said in Yana's native tongue, her voice pitched high and shaking.

The man's burrowed brow vanished as he lay eyes on her face, spotting the scarlet trail of blood down her chin. His grip loosened, and he ushered Maggie back to the entrance, near the metal detectors.

"Are you okay?" He shifted on his feet and didn't seem to know where to put his hands, clearly unaccustomed to dealing with an upset and bloody woman.

"No," Maggie wept, her voice cracking as she covered her face with her hands.

The guard cleared his throat and spoke with his colleague who held a radio in his hand, ready to alert backup if needed. The second guard shook his head and picked up a handheld device next to the door-shaped frame of the metal detector.

"I have to scan you," he said in a firm voice.

He motioned for Maggie to stand by the small x-ray machine for bags and other personal items and hovered the scanner over her body. It beeped around Maggie's hand, and the guard noted the bracelet around her wrist. She'd left her newly acquired gun back in Ashton's apartment. There was no way to get through security armed. All she had by way of weapons were her guile and her fists.

And that was all she needed.

"Personal belongings must go through the machine before we can let you in," the first guard advised.

"I don't have anything with me," Maggie snapped, turning to face him with her tear-streaked face.

The second guard returned the scanner and shared a look with his colleague, the meaning clear. He would deal with her. "Please, come with me," he said, offering a small and sympathetic smile.

At least her appearance worked on one of them. Maggie allowed the guard to lead her through an open door to the right, whimpering as they entered the front-of-house section of the consulate with a line of glass-covered kiosks along one wall.

A few people stood at the various kiosks, filling out forms and speaking in Russian to members of staff, much the same as it had been at the British Consulate. They all stopped when they spotted Maggie. One woman let out an audible gasp.

The guard took Maggie to a row of seats and sat her down with a gentle push. "What happened?" he asked.

"I," Maggie said, pausing to add a well-timed sniffle, "have been robbed."

"You poor thing," said an elderly woman, listening in from a few seats down.

Maggie let out a burst of tears at the woman's kind words and tilted her head back in despair. A camera was stationed in the middle of the high ceiling, allowing those watching to get a full view of the entire room.

"Someone robbed me, and I don't know what do to," she continued, louder this time for the audio on the camera feed. All eyes were on her, and Yana was making quite the scene.

A voice called through the man's radio asking for him to check in.

He turned away from Maggie and lowered his voice. "We have a hysterical woman claiming she was mugged."

Maggie's eye twitched at the word 'hysterical,' a term men liked to throw around whenever a woman showed any display of unhappiness, anger, or distress. The guard was lucky she was undercover, or she would have shown him *exactly* what hysterical meant.

At the end of the row of kiosks, a door opened and distracted Maggie from her temporary rage. Maggie took a deep, shaking breath as another man walked over to them.

His gait said military, his gray eyes trained on her as he took in the situation.

Maggie did some assessing of her own. Six foot one. A lean, yet powerful build. Agile footing. A gun concealed under his suit jacket. His posture was confident and full of authority. Maggie was willing to bet he was head of security.

"Hello, Madam. My name is Aleksandar Petrov. Would you come with me?"

Yana flinched as he reached for her. "Where?"

Aleksandar pulled his hand back and bent down on one knee, lowering himself to her level like he was talking to a small child.

"I understand that you have been in an altercation. Please come with me to my office so we can get you cleaned up and take your statement."

Maggie sniffed and wiped at her tear-filled eyes. Aleksandar offered a small smile that softened his otherwise harsh face, his nose, jaw, and cheekbones a collection of sharp angles. He kept his dark brown hair long and tied back smartly from his face in a tight ponytail.

"Go with him, dear," said the elderly woman with an encouraging nod. "He'll make sure you're okay and looked after." She tutted and shook her head. "Americans. Stealing from a young, helpless girl."

Maggie was many things, but helpless wasn't one of them.

She looked from the woman to Aleksandar, showing

Yana's trepidation before finally agreeing. "Okay," she said, hugging herself.

"Right this way," said Aleksandar. They left the guard to return to his post by the door while Aleksandar led Maggie deeper into the large building. Maggie kept an eye on the cameras, instinct keeping her face turned to avoid a direct image. Not that it mattered. Her face on their CCTV was the least of her worries as she followed Aleksandar up a set of marble stairs and further into enemy territory.

Committing each step to memory, Maggie kept an eye out for anything out of the ordinary. For anything that might indicate a higher level of security.

Nothing.

The hallway on the first floor was like a fancy five-star hotel, lavishly decorated to impress visitors, no doubt. Their footsteps were muffled thanks to a pristine cream carpet, the walls covered in matching wallpaper veined with gold designs and large paintings surrounded by gilded frames.

They turned a corner, and Aleksandar stopped by the next door. He swiped a card across the reader, and the locks clicked open. "Ladies first," he said.

Maggie stepped inside, Yana careful not to touch Aleksandar as she entered past him. He followed, closing the door behind him, and she flinched at the noise.

"It's okay." Aleksandar held his palms out as if in surrender. "You're safe here."

He gestured for Yana to take the seat across from a maple desk and she complied, shuddering as the tears subsided. The room was much like any other office, computer, shelves filled with folders and files, a well-watered plant by the window. For all the office said, Aleksandar could have been an insurance salesman.

Before sitting down, Aleksandar walked into a connecting bathroom and came back out with a damp towel. "Are you hurt?" he asked, handing the towel over and examining her from a distance.

Maggie dabbed at her mouth and winced for good measure. "More shaken than anything else," she replied, voice meek.

"Nothing appears to be broken," he concluded, sitting down across from her once satisfied that her wounds were superficial. "Your face and neck will bruise, though. I'll call and get a doctor to examine you, just in case."

"Okay." Maggie made sure to leave a smear of blood at the corner of her mouth to distract him. The more Aleksandar saw her as a victim, as a scared and defenseless young woman in a big, strange city, the better.

"What's your name?" he asked, moving the mouse of his computer and typing in his password.

"Yana. Yana Kostina."

Aleksandar typed her false name into what Maggie assumed was an incident report. "Where are you from, Yana?"

Maggie cleared her throat, making a show of discomfort as she spoke. "Cherepovets."

"I have family there."

Maggie stayed quiet. Small talk was a dangerous route for her to take. Digging too much into the past of an alias led to slip-ups, and she played on Yana's shock and fear to avoid any chitchat about a hometown she'd never visited.

"Yana, can you tell me what happened to you?" Aleksandar asked, repeating her name to ground her in the moment and calm her, a tactic she'd used before when dealing with people riddled with fear or shock.

"I was robbed." Maggie waved her hand in front of her face like she was about to cry again.

"It's okay," Aleksandar soothed. "Let's take it slow and start from the beginning. What brought you to New York?"

"I'm an art director at a gallery back home. Nothing big, but our latest exhibition got a glowing write up in the Media Center," she said in Yana's nervous prattling, having checked the name of the local newspaper in Cherepovets the night before. "I came here to visit the Guggenheim."

Aleksandar stopped typing and clasped his hands, giving Yana his full attention. "Can you believe I've been here nearly nine years and have yet to visit?"

Yana sat up straighter and met his eyes. She couldn't resist a discussion about art, even after what happened to her. Her true passion was a safe place, and much easier to discuss than her supposed mugging.

"Oh, but you must. They have the most comprehensive exhibition of Russian art outside of the homeland. Icons like the Virgin of Vladimir. Collections amassed by Peter and Catherine the Great. Shchukin and Morozov. Avant-Garde. Even Post-Soviet pieces." Maggie lowered her head and picked at her thumbnail, one of Yana's nervous ticks. "Not that I got to see any of it."

Aleksandar gave her some time to compose herself before asking the inevitable. "Is that where it happened?"

She nodded. "It all happened so fast."

"Why didn't you go to the police?"

"Would you? I watch the news. They don't like us, and I don't trust them," she said, not having to clarify who *they* were.

"You did the right thing." Aleksandar went back to his computer. More typing. "We'll do everything we can to find the ones who did this to you."

"And my things?"

"I wouldn't get my hopes up, Ms. Kostina. New York is a very big place, and even if we do arrest the ones responsible, your belongings will most likely be long gone."

Maggie sniffed, eyes filling with tears again. "They took everything. My phone, my money, the key to my hotel room."

"We can help you with all of that. Now, do you have anything to confirm your identity and citizenship, Ms.

Kostina? It's just a security precaution," he added when she frowned at his request.

"I have my passport." Maggie pulled out the counterfeit ID and passed it over.

Aleksandar checked inside, his eyes flitting between Maggie and the photo of Yana. "If someone stole your bag, how do you still have your passport?"

"My father told me to keep it in my pocket. He was always going on about American muggers and New York's dangerous streets. I didn't really believe what he said, but I did as he asked." Maggie rubbed at her throat again, her voice scratchy as she spoke and getting worse. "I can't believe he was right."

"Do you want a drink?" Aleksandar asked.

"Please," she rasped, coughing.

Aleksandar opened the door to a little fridge by his desk and brought out a cool bottle of water, condensation dripping down the plastic.

"Could I have something hot?" Maggie leaned her head to one side to show off the bruising on her neck. "My throat hurts from where they grabbed me."

Muscles twitched on Aleksandar's jaw as he peered at the handy work of the supposed muggers, a dark look sweeping past his eyes. "Of course. Stay here, and I'll be back in one moment with some coffee."

"Thank you," said Maggie with a weak smile. "You've been very kind."

Maggie waited until the door clicked shut behind him

and dashed from her seat to Aleksandar's. Grabbing the mouse, she caught the computer before the screensaver locked her out.

"Kind, but stupid."

Men always underestimated women. While irritating to the highest degree, the predictability of the phenomenon was useful and had helped Maggie during missions more than any other weapon. Being overlooked came with advantages, and she exploited them to the fullest.

A tab was already open on Aleksandar's computer, and she double clicked it into full-screen. Live video footage blinked back at her, a grid of squares for each camera in the building and the outside perimeter. Aleksandar himself came into view at the top left, heading down the hall and into what looked like a staffroom where a few people waited in line for coffee from a vending machine.

Scanning each square, Maggie searched for her target. Emily Wallace was somewhere inside, for now, and she needed to move before the head of security came back. Aleksandar would raise the alarm the moment he found Yana missing. Maggie needed to find Emily and get the hell out of there before that happened, which didn't leave her much time.

A feed at the bottom caught her attention. While not overtly different from the other rows of doors, two guards stood sentry outside. Something important must lay inside.

Or someone.

Using the feeds to plot the route to the guarded door, Maggie slipped out of the office and hurried down the corridor in the opposite direction from Aleksandar's coffee run.

The hallways were deserted. The upper floors of consulates weren't generally used by the public. The door in question lay on the ground floor at the back of the building. Maggie took a different set of stairs down to avoid the guards by the front entrance. They would intercept her on sight if seen without a chaperone.

With pricked ears, Maggie crept down the steps.

Pressing against the wall, Maggie inched to the corner and risked a glance around the edge towards what she hoped was Emily's prison. The guards were still there, postures rigid and alert despite their bored expressions. Professionals.

Maggie was no amateur, either, and without wasting another second, she rounded the corner into plain sight.

"Help," she called, running towards them and looking back over her shoulder like she was being chased. "Please, you have to help me."

"What's wrong?" The man stepped forward, abandoning his post.

"You can't be down here." The woman reached inside

her suit jacket, seeming unimpressed with Maggie's performance.

"He's going to kill me!" Maggie voice was wild with fear.

The male guard reached out to her, but the female guard held him back as she scrutinized Maggie with narrowed eyes.

"He's got Aleksandar," Maggie cried as she grew closer, not stopping.

Both guards paused at that and shared an alarmed look. It didn't matter if either of them believed her. All Maggie needed was a precious few seconds of distraction to bridge the gap between them.

Maggie sprung into the air and shot out her leg, catching the man in the temple with a roundhouse kick. The steel toecap on her boots worked like a charm, and he crumpled to the floor. His eyes rolled to the back of his head before he even registered her attack.

The woman wasn't so slow.

What Maggie thought was a gun, turned out to be a baton. The guard flicked it out to its full length and swung it at Maggie like her head was a piñata.

Maggie ducked just in time and slammed her fist into the woman's gut. The guard doubled over, the baton traveling with her momentum and catching Maggie in the arm with a sickening *thwack*.

The pain elicited a sharp hiss, and Maggie grabbed the bottom of the baton, yanking it forward. The guard stumbled, unable to catch her footing, and Maggie clipped her on the chin with an uppercut. Her head snapped back, and she staggered back, giving Maggie enough room to kick the woman square in the chest, sending her crashing back into the door.

The impact left a dent in the wood, and as the guard struggled to get back to her feet, Maggie caught her with a right hook and sent the woman to the floor beside her partner.

Listening for signs of new arrivals, Maggie turned the handle to the door. It didn't budge.

"Shit."

An electronic reader was positioned on the wall next to the door, the light red. Remembering Aleksandar's card, Maggie bent and rummaged through the unconscious guards' pockets. She found a keycard in the man's jacket and swiped it through the reader. The light switched from red to green, and Maggie entered.

"Who are you?"

Emily Wallace stood up, abandoning the couch that took up most of the little box room. There were no windows, and empty bottles of water lay scattered on the carpet. They'd kept Emily there for a while.

"A friend." Maggie checked the hall for signs of back-up. The coast was clear, for now.

Emily's braids fell over one shoulder, dark eyes innocent yet untrusting. "You're British," she said, clearly expecting another Russian.

"Well spotted."

Emily crossed her arms. "I don't know you." Her blue dress sparkled underneath an oversized hoodie, which Maggie suspected belonged to one of her captors. Black leggings covered her legs, ending in a pair of well-loved Converse on her feet.

"I'm here to rescue you," Maggie said, her patience thinning.

Emily exhaled in relief. "Did my mom send you?"

"We don't have time to talk." Maggie reached out her hand. "Come with me. Now."

Maggie's sharp tone must have frightened the girl. She could see the cogs working in Emily's head, wondering if she could trust this stranger. One of many she must have come into contact since her abduction.

"If you prefer, you can stay here." Maggie shrugged. "Either way, I've got to go."

That did it. Emily reached out and took Maggie's hand, letting her pull her out of the room and into the hallway.

"Don't mind them," Maggie said, as she stepped over the guards and scooped up the woman's baton along the way.

Emily looked back at them, her short legs working double time to keep up with Maggie's pace. "Did you do that?"

Maggie shushed her. "Stay quiet."

Then the alarm began. A high-pitched wail screeched

throughout the hallway, screaming like a banshee in Maggie's ears.

"Bollocks," she swore, dragging Emily to the staircase.

Emily dug her heels. "Shouldn't we be running out the front door?"

"Quiet," Maggie hissed. "If they catch us, the only way we're leaving this building is in a body bag. Got it?"

Emily nodded, eyes wide.

"Good, now do as I say, and we might make it out of this mess alive." Maggie forced a smile as her mind raced through her plans. She unclasped Yana's bracelet and fastened it around Emily's slender wrist.

"What's that for?"

"It's a tracker. If we get split up, I can find you." Not that Maggie intended to lose sight of Emily. The bracelet was strictly a safeguard for the worst-case scenario.

They traveled back upstairs and headed towards the front of the building. A flurry of confused and alarmed voices echoed down the hallway, originating around the corner. Lockdown protocols would already be in place. The guards would secure civilians in offices and safe rooms while the advanced security team searched the building to eliminate the imminent threat.

At the end of the hallway, Maggie led Emily into a room on their left and closed the door.

The lounge was brightly lit from the sun shining through the large windows and was likely used for meeting and entertaining foreign dignitaries. Plush sofas sat around well-polished tables with decanters of amber liquid and crystal glasses arranged like centerpieces. Ornate paintings hung from the walls, and portraits of stern-looking nobles stared down at them with disapproving eyes.

Marching footsteps approached outside the door, and Maggie's heart leapt in her chest.

Darting her eyes over the room, she narrowed in on the grand piano in the corner. "Help me move this," she ordered Emily, kicking the brakes up from the wheels of each leg.

Emily complied as the racket through the door grew louder. The handle on the door began to turn, and Maggie shoved the piano the last few feet just in time to stop it from opening.

The handle moved to no avail. Muffled Russian curses penetrated the door. The wood shuddered as someone rammed their shoulder into the door, trying to break it down. Maggie kicked down the brakes on the piano and stepped back. It should hold them off long enough.

Shoulders were replaced with feet, and the door rattled in its frame.

Emily's hands shook, and Maggie patted her shoulder. "They won't get in," she assured the frightened girl.

"Get the axe," called a rough voice in Russian.

Well shit.

It was time to get a move on.

The slamming grew louder and more violent as more guards joined the fray.

"It's a dead end," Emily squealed, circling the room. "We're trapped."

"Not quite." Maggie moved to the windows and peered outside. It was risky, but it was their best shot at getting out unnoticed. Grabbing the curtains draping to the floor, she wrapped her hand in the thick fabric. Maggie sucked in a breath and punched her covered fist through the window. The glass shattered to the floor around them like sharp-edged diamonds.

Clearing the rest of the glass away with her boot, Maggie swung her leg out over the window pane. No guards were outside the building yet, too concerned about who was inside rather than out.

Wind whistled past her and brushed her hair from her face. It wasn't a huge drop to the sidewalk, but it was enough to break or sprain an ankle if you landed wrong. Worse if you failed to land on your feet at all.

"Where are you going?" Emily flinched as the first blow from the axe collided with the door.

"I think we've overstayed our welcome." Maggie propped both feet on the window ledge. "Now watch what I do. I need you to copy me, okay?"

A tear slipped down the girl's cheek, panic threatening to take over.

Maggie clicked her fingers. "Emily, do you hear me? I need you to follow exactly what I do."

Emily nodded, wiping her face with the overlong sleeve of her hoodie.

The scaffolding framing the building next door jutted out four feet away. It was a simple jump, but Maggie couldn't risk Emily falling. Especially given how shaken she was.

Another crash sounded against the door, a crack forming down the center as the axe chipped away at the wood piece by piece.

Careful of the glass, Maggie gripped the window frame to steady herself before moving. With her feet planted securely on the ledge, she inched over and reached out for the stone pillar framing the window. The ledge was barely wide enough for her foot, and she shuffled across to the edge of the consulate building. Maggie reached for the corner pole of the scaffolding next door and swung herself around until her feet found purchase on the wooden slate walkway.

Emily's head bobbed out from the window. "I can't do that."

"Yes, you can," said Maggie. "You have to."

Yelling echoed out of the window along with the collision of sharpened metal on wood. "They're breaking through!"

"Come on," Maggie urged. They were losing precious time. "Your mother's waiting on you."

Though Maggie didn't even know her mother's name, the white lie was enough for Emily. A steely look passed over her eyes, and she clenched a determined jaw.

"Take your time," said Maggie as the girl stepped out

onto the ledge. "Keep your eyes on your feet, but don't look down any further."

Emily was painfully slow, but Maggie refrained from rushing her. "That's it," she encouraged, checking behind her for any signs of the workmen. Drills and hammering rang from above amid light-hearted chatter. Most of them were on the upper levels, but she'd be ready if they encountered any stragglers who tried to stop them or called attention to their presence.

A loud crash announced the shattering of the door from inside, and the guards' voices floated clear as crystal out the window.

"It's blocked. There's a fucking piano."

"Climb over it."

Emily heard it too, and she moved faster towards the scaffolding.

Maggie reached out her arms. "Almost there."

Emily fumbled forward. Her foot snagged and missed the ledge, falling out from under her. She screamed as she fell back into nothing but thin air.

Maggie dove out, using the corner rail of the scaffolding to steady her, and grabbed the scruff of Emily's hoodie. A jolt of pain ran up her arm as she bore the weight of Emily, her muscles burning under the strain of the hanging girl.

Emily kicked and flailed in panic, but Maggie dug her fingers into the fabric and hoisted her up with everything she had. When Emily cleared the edge, Maggie pulled herself onto the scaffolding, and they fell back into the safety of the walkway. "I've got you," panted Maggie. "You're safe."

It was the second lie she told Emily Wallace that day.

The danger was far from over.

Chapter 6

Maggie led Emily down the street from the consulate and turned onto 5th Avenue when the first group of Russians sped out the front door. The gates drew open, and a detail of three SUVs with tinted windows pulled onto the road.

The traffic lights turned red, and Maggie and Emily weaved between vehicles as they crossed the road, ducking behind a delivery van to stay out of view. Scurrying across to the sidewalk, Maggie risked a glance as the lights flicked to green and the traffic crawled forward through the crowded city streets.

The SUVs growled with impatience at their red light, waiting with blinkers flashing and ready to give chase.

"We need to get off the street." Maggie scanned the buildings, connected the sights to the map of New York she'd memorized. The lavish Cooper-Hewitt museum sat directly across from them, once the mansion of industrialist Andrew Carnegie.

Across from the mansion stood the Church of Heavenly Rest, its neo-gothic arches and foreboding presence less than welcoming. Maggie wouldn't seek sanctuary there. The church's very name seemed like a bad omen.

Maggie forced her pace to slow to a brisk walk and kept Emily close as they continued down the street. A row of parked cars lined their left, the brick wall that encased Central Park by their right.

The park.

"This way," Maggie steered Emily past a hotdog cart and into the eastern entrance of Central Park.

The path through the park led them in the opposite direction of the British Consulate, but the direct route was too open. Too dangerous.

Two point three miles separated the consulates. Forty-seven minutes on foot. Less than that if running. It didn't sound long, but traveling the forty or so blocks would be tricky under normal situations, but with a scared kid, mounting morning sickness, and the Russians close behind, it felt as impossible right then as running the New York City marathon.

Taking 3rd Avenue would be the fastest, but not necessarily the wisest, route. Yet the longer Maggie kept Emily Wallace out on the streets, the longer the enemy had to track them down and kill them both.

That meant taking an alternative route.

The park was busier than Maggie expected on a weekday afternoon. A cluster of school kids huddled around a teacher who bellowed for them to gather around and get into pairs. The wind rustled through the trees and swept along the early fallen leaves that blanketed the pathways, rushing past Maggie's feet like a river of red and gold.

A vendor selling cheesy t-shirts and hats shouted his wares from the corner by the entrance. A cluster of straggling school kids harassed him, asking how much each t-shirt cost when the sign said everything was ten dollars.

"This isn't worth ten bucks," said a young haggler. "I'll give you five for it."

"Look, kid quit bustin' my balls. If the sign says ten, it's ten."

Maggie brushed past the little stand and swiped an *I heart NYC* shirt and hat. The kids kept the vendor occupied, and a smile tugged at her lips, wondering if her own child would be full of mischief.

"Put these on." She handed the clothes to Emily and tossed the girl's oversized hoodie into a nearby trash can. Maggie shrugged out of her cardigan and added it to the pile, along with her short-haired wig.

"Who are you?" Emily asked. "Some kind of Jane Bond?"

"No," Maggie replied, running a hand through her real hair. "I like my martinis stirred."

Emily simply frowned.

Tires screeched and sent Maggie's heart to her throat. Grabbing Emily, they crossed East Drive, a road that allowed cars to drive through the park, and slunk into Bridle Path which lay parallel to it. They crouched behind a set of bushes that Autumn had visited early, leaving little gaps where the leaves had already fallen.

Two of the SUVs pulled into the park, barely slowing for pedestrians who rushed to avoid being hit.

The drivers slammed on the brakes, which squealed like the school children Maggie had seen before. The vehicles stopped a mere ten yards from Maggie and Emily's hiding spot, and Aleksandar emerged from the first one, followed closely by his men. He barked out orders, sending a group north on foot and directing the second SUV southbound down the drive. The third car was nowhere to be seen.

The head of security scanned the area by the first SUV, his body taught with barely controlled rage. Maggie had penetrated his fortress and stolen his witness, which not only undermined him and his job, but the country he served, too. Aleksandar was out for blood.

Unfortunately for him, Maggie was *not* easy prey.

"Come on," she whispered, helping Emily up. "We need to go."

Keeping hidden, they traveled up a set of stone steps and reached the Shuman Running Track which ran the circumference of the large man-made stretch of water. Beyond, the reservoir stretched out, taking center stage in New York's oasis, acting as a reprieve to the grimy urban streets and imposing gray skyscrapers. The sun glittered off the surface and winked back at them.

It was a beautiful sight, but Maggie and Emily couldn't stop and stare. Maggie nodded to her charge as a group of middle-aged runners approached, and together they joined in the pack, heading south towards the bottom of the reservoir.

"What will happen if they catch us?" Emily asked, puffing.

"It won't come to that." Maggie kept her eyes trained for any signs they'd been found. The park was a big place, but Aleksandar had a whole crew of trained professionals after them.

Beads of sweat formed across Maggie's forehead as she ran. September in New York City wasn't like London, where the cold swooped in like an unwelcome house guest who stayed until Spring. The last of the Summer's sun bore down on them with each step, with only the breeze of the wind offering a slight reprieve.

Five minutes later, the track opened out, and they arrived at the south gate house. The stone building looked out into the park, a picturesque bridge rested at the foot of the main steps. But that wasn't what caught Maggie's attention.

Two men in suits spotted her and Emily from the footpath below. The men broke into a run the second they saw their targets, mouthing into earpieces, jackets flapping in the wind.

"Run!" Maggie urged Emily forward, back onto the running track. A cluster of tourists had stopped by the water to feed a family of ducks with torn pieces of pretzels, taking snaps of the little birds on their cellphones.

Maggie barged into them and cleared a gap for Emily, not stopping to explain. A few of the tourists fell into each other amid their rabble of complaints and cries, but Maggie didn't care. They'd create a diversion, blocking their pursuers, even if only for a couple of moments. Those precious seconds could be the difference between life and death.

Emily winced and gripped the side of her waist. "I can't keep running."

"You must," Maggie said, scooping her arm through Emily's and forcing her to move. She risked a glance behind them to see the men in suits. Two had become four, a second pair of Russians closing in quick.

They were fast. Faster than Emily.

Maggie grit her teeth and checked that the baton she'd stolen was still tucked in her waistband. It wouldn't do much against a set of guns, but it was better than nothing. As they ran, Maggie used innocent passersby as human shields and hoped the Russians wouldn't risk taking out a civilian. If only to avoid a very public international incident.

But no matter what Maggie tried, the pounding foot-steps and angry shouts drew closer. Maggie tugged on Emily's arm and merged them back onto Bridle Path.

"They're too fast. There's too many of them," cried Emily between pants. She was getting slower, the adrenaline from her fear losing the battle against her fatigue.

Maggie closed her eyes and focused on the map she studied on the flight over. The grid system made New York easier to navigate than most cities. They were at the bottom of the reservoir now, which put them five or six blocks south of the Russian Consulate.

"Left," said Maggie, warning Emily before they made the turn. There was no direct pathway from their position, causing them to barge through a thicket of trees and bushes. Bare branches snagged at Maggie's clothes, but she surged on, holding tight to Emily's hand.

"They're right behind us," Emily warned.

Maggie could hear their panting breathes, much more controlled than Emily's labored gasps. Like Maggie, the Russians could keep this pace for miles. They wouldn't slow down. They wouldn't stop. Not until they caught their targets. Not until she and Emily were dead.

"Jump!" Maggie yelled when the thicket stopped. She didn't wait for Emily to comply. Instead, she gripped the girl's hand tighter and pulled Emily over the edge of the bushes and dropped down into the middle of a street.

Emily screamed, but the drop wasn't far. She landed hard, tearing the thin material of her leggings and skinning her knees. Maggie pulled her up and crossed the street. Emily's injuries could wait. First, she had to keep the girl alive.

The 85th Street Transverse veined through the middle of Central Park, snaking from East 85th Street on one side, to West 86th on the other. Right smack in the middle of said street was the 22nd Precinct Police Station, which was exactly where Maggie was headed.

Two officers stood by the front gates of the precinct. While Maggie doubted the NYPD's finest boys in blue would be a match for Aleksandar's men, she was desperate and out of options.

Above them, ruffling came from the bushes, and the first of the gang of Russians followed them into the street.

Maggie and Emily hurried towards the police, and Maggie slipped on a mask of terrified innocence. "Officers! There are men following us, and they have guns. They tried to force us into the back of a van."

One of the officers called for backup on his radio and stepped in front of Maggie and Emily, heading towards the approaching Russian security operatives.

The officer's partner turned to Maggie and opened the gate. "Ma'am, you and the girl go inside and stay there until it's safe."

"Thank you," Maggie said, stepping through the gates with an arm over Emily's shoulders. She backtracked as soon as the officer ran to meet his partner, and left the precinct as five more policemen and women came to help their colleagues.

The police couldn't protect them, but they did make for a good distraction while Maggie and Emily hurried down the street and headed towards the Upper West Side.

Chapter 7

By the time they emerged from Central Park, Maggie had come to a dangerous conclusion: Emily wouldn't last. Her feet dragged more with each step, her breathing grew labored, and her face winced with each step from the stitch in her side.

Maggie checked over her shoulder. Aleksandar and his men were nowhere to be seen, but that didn't mean they weren't close. Maggie needed to get Emily off the streets and out of sight as soon as possible.

Which meant the subway.

They walked all the way to the end of the block to use the crosswalk to avoid unwanted attention. Cops were everywhere, and no matter Maggie's views on the ridiculousness of ticketing for jaywalking, the last thing they needed was to get stopped and charged for being in a hurry.

The 86th Street station was closest, and Maggie and Emily merged with the crowd as they traveled to the terminal. Paying for two tickets with fresh bills, she and Emily waited for the C train and hopped on. Maggie double checked the lines depicted on the car's interior once they'd found a seat. Five stops and they'd be at 42nd Street. From there, the E train would take them to Lexington Avenue, leaving them a short two-minute walk from the British Consulate.

The car filled up fast, and Maggie kept an eye on each passenger who stepped inside, evaluating their threat level before moving on to the next. None of them were Aleksandar's men.

Passengers squeezed into Maggie's car like sardines even though the adjacent car lay empty. Having visited the city several times, Maggie knew that meant the smell was unbearable, thanks to what was usually vomit, excrement, or some unforgiveable combination of the two.

City life had its glamorous side, but public transport wasn't one of them.

Maggie turned to Emily, checking her red knees. The blood had stopped, but the open skin needed to be cleaned. "How are you holding up?"

Emily shrugged and wrapped her arms around her waist. Fear lined her young face, the remnants of childhood still in her round cheeks. She was holding up okay, all things considered. Homework and petty arguments with friends should be the extent of worries for a girl so young. Not running for her life.

If the Russians had their way, Emily wouldn't live to see another sunrise. A dark thought shadowed Maggie's thoughts, and her nails dug into her palms.

"Emily did anyone..." Maggie stopped, trying to find the right words.

"Touch me?" Emily finished for her. She shook her head. "No."

Maggie's tense muscles relaxed a little, grateful for that one small miracle at least. Emily seemed to calm a little while talking, so Maggie kept her chatting.

"How old are you?"

"Twelve, but I'll be thirteen in a few weeks."

"A teenager. Your mom must have her hands full." The idea of having an infant—never mind a teen—hit Maggie like a ton of bricks. Emily was her responsibility right now, but taking care of the life growing inside her would be a full-time job. Was she ready for that? Was Leon? A pang of guilt tugged at her heart.

She should tell him. As soon as the mission was over.

Emily sighed. "Yeah, I'm getting old."

"I know the feeling." Maggie grinned. "I like your dress."

"I don't." Emily groaned. "My mom made me wear it for the party. I still wore my Chucks, though." The hint of a mischievous grin tugged at the corner of her lips.

Maggie nudged her. "Rebel. What was the party for?"

"Some boring thing for some boring colleague of my mom's. She's a human rights lawyer."

Which explained why Emily found herself at a party with a UN official. It wasn't lost on Maggie that Emily could tell her more than Jonathan Cole and Danielle Hawkins had bothered to share.

"And you saw something?" Maggie asked. "Something bad."

Tears filled Emily's eyes. "Yes."

Maggie wiped Emily's eyes dry with the sleeve of her shirt. While Maggie's curiosity about the assassination was strong, she didn't want to upset her charge. Especially not in public with prying eyes.

"Do you work for the UN, too?" Emily asked.

Maggie shook her head and filed the tidbits of information she'd learned with what else she knew.

"But you were hired to come get me?"

"Something like that," Maggie admitted. Even with the panic and deadly situation, she found herself in, Emily didn't miss much. Her mother had raised her well, and although Maggie had been trained to keep charges at an emotional distance, she couldn't help but warm to the girl.

"I don't even know your name," Emily said.

"I'm Yan—" Maggie stopped. "My name is Maggie."

"Maggie, do you think I can go home now? I wanna see my parents."

"Soon." Maggie took Emily's hand and gave it a squeeze.

The car slowed down for the first stop at 81st Street, right by the Museum of Natural History. People got on and off, a mixture of bored looking locals and excited tourists trying out the famed underground system for the first time.

Four more stops, a line switch, then another four stops. They'd both be safe soon, and Maggie could return home to deal with her own predicament. So many things were about to change.

Just as the doors pinged in warning that they were about to close, three men in suits squeezed through in time before the train set off again.

Maggie tensed and swore under her breath. Aleksandar headed towards them, flanked by two men, with a sneer on his face.

There was nowhere to run. Nowhere to hide.

They were locked in until the next stop.

"Thanks for getting me out of there," Emily said, who hadn't noticed the approaching Russians.

"You're very welcome." Maggie stood and reached for her waistband. "It's all part of the job."

Emily stared up at her. "What *is* your job?"

Maggie grabbed the baton and flicked it open.

"To keep you safe."

Chapter 8

Maggie held out her hand. Emily took it without question and gasped when she spotted the Suits heading toward them. Aleksandar and his men moved with a singular focus, their eyes trained on Emily.

"Come on," Maggie said, leading Emily down the packed aisle. She opened the doors separating one car from the next and slipped through the gap, the Russians closing in behind them.

Her heartbeat pounded loud in Maggie's ears with each step. Small, wall-mounted lights flew past the windows in a blur. They couldn't get out. Not until the next stop, and by then it could be too late.

They carried on from the empty, foul-smelling car and through to a third which was packed with people. Emily stumbled forward, tripping over their fellow passengers' feet and shopping bags.

Maggie closed her eyes when she spotted the problem, hitting a dead end sooner than expected. It was the last car on the train. "Shit."

"Maggie," Emily whimpered, as the car door opened and Aleksandar stepped inside with his goons. She pointed to the man in charge. "He's the one who took me."

There was no escape, and Maggie prepared herself for the inevitable.

"Go to the far corner and crouch behind the seats. Cover yourself as best you can and don't move." It was the best Maggie could do for now.

Emily complied and ran to the very back of the car. Maggie straightened her spine and stared down her opponents.

The air changed, and the passengers seemed to sense something was wrong. They looked up from their phones and stopped talking to their partners, each searching for the cause of their instinctual unease.

Aleksandar cleared his throat. "Ladies and gentlemen, this car is now closed to the public. Move to another car. Now."

New Yorkers didn't need to be told twice. Trouble was coming, and no one wanted to be around to get caught in the crossfire. There was a flurry of rustled fabric, zipping bags, and a crescendo of footsteps as the passengers hurried past Aleksandar and into the next car.

A young man in Timberland boots and a hoodie

stopped by Maggie as the others left. "Yo, ma'am, these guys don't look so happy to see you. Do you need help?"

Maggie kept her attention on the Russians. "They're the ones who're going to need help."

One of the goons lunged for her then, and the would-be-Samaritan sprung forward before Maggie could stop him. The goon dodged his uppercut with ease and took him down with a roundhouse kick that caught the young man's temple.

Aleksandar's laughter echoed through the empty car as the civilian crumpled to the floor. "All you're doing is slowing us down. You cannot stop the inevitable end."

Maggie straightened and twirled the handle of the baton, keeping it loose in her dexterous hands. "If you want the girl, you're going to have to go through me."

Aleksandar arched an eyebrow. "As you wish."

The three men charged forward, and Maggie waited until they were almost upon her. Without a second to spare, she leapt up and grabbed the metal bar above her. Using the momentum to her advantage, she swung forward and kicked the first man square in the chest.

The blow landed with an encouraging *whoosh* as the air knocked from his lungs. The man reeled back, colliding into Aleksandar. The pair stumbled and fell to the dirty floor in a pile of tangled limbs.

Maggie released the grab bar and dropped to her feet. But the third guard was there in an instant. He clipped

Maggie across the face with his fist, quicker than she could raise her hands in defense.

Something wet trickled from her nose, and Maggie tasted a familiar coppery tang on her lips. A wave of anger rushed through her. No one drew blood and got away with it.

Maggie ducked under the man's next jab and swung her baton. The weapon caught the man at the side of his face with a satisfying *crunch*. Spittle, blood, and teeth flew from his mouth and spattered across the glass window. He collapsed, clutching his face, and Maggie turned in time to find Aleksandar and his comrade clambering back to their feet.

The guard reached for the gun at his side. Maggie couldn't have him shooting off rounds in the small subway car. She lashed out with her baton, swinging it past his arm, hitting him hard enough to snap bone in two. A kick in the solar plexus sent him careening to the floor with his colleague, evening the playing field to one on one.

Hands grabbed Maggie's hair and pulled her back with enough force to send her stumbling back. Strands ripped from her roots, and she hissed in pain as Aleksandar dragged her towards him.

She pivoted to try and free herself, but the man's grip was unrelenting. Maggie kicked for his groin, but Aleksandar had more experience than his staff and easily dodged the strike.

The back of his hand smacked against her jaw and

sent her head spinning from the impact. He was strong. Much stronger than Maggie.

A fist caught her in the same spot, sending a second surge of pain through her jaw that rattled her teeth. Maggie blinked away the black dots in her vision and focused on her opponent.

One of the fallen guards—the one with the broken arm —was speaking in rapid-fire Russian into his radio, calling for help. But Maggie had no time to stop him, forced to counter a third attack from Aleksandar.

He aimed a brutal kick towards Maggie's stomach, and a surge of maternal fear pulsed through her. She flung out her arm, the clumsy block hurting just as much as taking the hit. Acute stabs of pain ran up her arm, causing her to drop her weapon, but at least the blow missed its intended target.

She fell back a step and eyed her enemy. Aleksandar never spoke. No jibes. No pompous shit talk. No gloating. He was all business, and he was winning.

Maggie couldn't allow that.

Her head ached and, from the throbbing in her gums, she was certain she was going to need some dental work. Spitting out a mouthful of blood, Maggie reset her stance and focused on her opponent's movements, looking for something, *anything*, she could use to turn the tide on their battle.

Aleksandar faked left and landed another sickening blow, sending Maggie reeling to the floor before she even realized she misjudged his target. Adrenaline coursed through her, clogging her mind and leaving her gasping for air as the shock of the punch subsided and the pain registered.

Her eyes watered. Aleksandar's blurry form loomed over her like a towering skyscraper, ready to finish her off with one final hit.

A high-pitched cry pierced the subway car, and Maggie gasped as little Emily charged the Russian. She swung the dropped baton like a baseball bat and smashed it with all her might against the back of Aleksandar's head.

Aleksandar swayed and placed a hand over the strike point, his fingers coming away slick with blood. His faced hardened and knuckles cracked in his tight fists.

Maggie gaped at the head of security, amazed he was still standing.

"Maggie," Emily cried, tossing the baton her way.

"Bitch," Aleksandar swore, reaching for Emily.

Getting to her feet, Maggie raced along the subway seats and jumped back to the floor, separating Emily and the Russian. Aleksandar threw another punch, the blow to his head making his movements sluggish.

Which only accentuated Maggie's sole advantage: her speed.

Air whooshed past her face as she dodged Aleksandar's punch. Quick as an alley cat, Maggie swung the baton, snapping several of the man's exposed ribs. He stumbled forward, a shout escaping his lips, and Maggie aimed a second blow for the same spot Emily had softened.

A sickening crunch proceeded a dull thud as Aleksandar collapsed to the ground.

"Are you okay?" Emily asked, running to Maggie.

"You shouldn't have stepped in," she chided.

"I got him good though," replied Emily with a sheepish smile.

That she had.

Maggie laughed as she slumped down onto a seat and wiped the sweat from her brow. It was a close one, and her head spun from the dizzying blows she'd sustained. "I don't know much about baseball, but I'd say that was a home run."

The train began to slow again, reaching its next stop. Maggie winced as she got up, using the handrail to keep her steady. One of the goons was still muttering into his radio on the floor, clutching his broken arm. A simple kick to the face put an end to his communications.

Maggie checked the good Samaritan on the way out, thankful to discover he was still breathing. He'd have one heck of a headache when he finally came to.

Staying on the train was out of the question now. It was time for plan B.

Chapter 9

Maggie battled the impulse to barge through the crowd. To push and shove anyone and everyone blocking their path. Each step felt like it took twice as long as it should, the brisk pace of New Yorkers too slow for her as she and Emily traveled through the station and out into West 72nd Street. Blending in was the best option. Running would get them noticed, and there was no telling where the rest of Aleksandar's team was.

It didn't take long for them to find out.

Brakes shrieked. Doors slammed.

Maggie snapped her head towards the sounds as one of the SUVs in Aleksandar's fleet pulled up from Central Park West. His team spilled from each side, and Maggie cursed herself for taking so long to shut up the man with the radio.

"Shit," Maggie hissed. "Run!"

Grabbing Emily, she high tailed it down the street in the opposite direction, heading towards Columbus Avenue.

"They must have called in our location," Maggie said, scanning the area for an escape route.

The Russians followed them on foot, the driver of the SUV blaring the horn at the traffic blocking his way.

Maggie cursed the lack of alleys, each of the buildings joined to the next, as she and Emily sprinted on. They approached the intersection with Columbus Ave, but something was wrong.

Her hearing perked up, and Maggie dug her heels into the ground, yanking Emily back just in time. A second SUV hurtled towards them from around the corner of the street. It bumped up over the sidewalk and crashed right where they'd been standing a split second before, blocking their path.

Maggie spun on her heels and dragged Emily back the way they came as more Russians rushed from the second vehicle to join the pursuit.

They were cornered from both ends.

"What are we going to do?" Emily cried, digging her nails into Maggie's hand. They were trapped.

The hum of an engine purred, growing louder as it approached. A motorbike. It wasn't anything special, an old Honda decked out with decals for a local pizza joint, but it might be enough.

Maggie made a silent apology to the delivery driver and hoped this wouldn't jeopardize their job. As the vehicle approached, Maggie stepped into its path and threw out her arm.

It caught the delivery guy's neck in a clothesline, and he flew from the seat. The motorcycle skidded along the road with bright sparks as metal met asphalt.

Emily ran after their escape vehicle. Maggie spared a quick second to make sure the delivery guy wasn't injured before following her charge. Hoisting the bike up, Maggie swung her leg over the seat and revved the engine. Emily wrapped her arms around Maggie's waist, hopping on behind her without having to be told.

A bang ricocheted off the stone walls of the surrounding buildings as one of the Russians fired a warning shot into the air. Pedestrians dispersed like a flock of scared sheep, and Maggie didn't stay around for the next bullet either.

She hit the road full throttle and sped down the street towards the second SUV. The driver spotted her and reversed off the sidewalk, backing into the street—much to the annoyance of a speeding taxi. Maggie dodged the approaching car, leaning into the turn and missing the back bumper with mere inches to spare.

Cars honked in anger as Maggie weaved between them. The smash of metal and glass suggested the SUVs weren't being overly careful in their pursuit, but Maggie didn't look back. She leaned down into the bike and picked up the pace.

Columbus Ave was a wide street with four lanes and ample room for the SUVs to bully their way through the traffic. Car brakes skidded behind them with a symphony of horns, the deep rumbling engines of the SUVs unrelenting and getting closer.

"Maggie," Emily warned, as one of the two vehicles came up from behind.

It bumped the back of the bike.

Emily squealed, tightening her grip on Maggie as she tried to steady the bike. The SUV bumped them again and jolted them forward. The rear fender cracked, and a piece fell off, crunching beneath the wheels of the SUV.

Checking her mirrors, Maggie swerved into the next lane and hit the brakes, slowing down to leave a gap between them and their hunters.

While the first SUV flew on past the bike, the second SUV caught on quick. They came into view from the rear, overtaking a cab on the lane to Maggie's right and forcing the car in front of them to speed up or be hit.

Three seconds later, the Russians were in line with the bike. Maggie risked a sideward glance and caught the driver spinning the wheel to the left.

The SUV crossed into Maggie's lane with a vicious screech. Maggie moved, inching as close to the opposite lane as she dared, and dodged a collision that would have sent her and Emily off the bike.

Two could play at that game.

Maggie kept pace with the SUV and reached for her baton. Keeping the motorbike steady with one hand and flipping the baton out with the other, Maggie shattered the driver's window. Most of the glass sprayed the driver, but a few errant pieces ricocheted back, cutting Maggie's cheek, but she didn't care.

The baton had done its job. A second jab of the weapon hit the driver with enough force to distract him from the road. By the time he noticed the parked garbage truck, it was too late. The SUV ran straight into the back of it in an explosion of shattered windows and burst trash bags.

A wicked grin spread across Maggie's face. One down. One to go.

They approached an intersection as the lights switched from green to red, and the surrounding cars slowed to stop. Maggie hit the gas.

"Hold on tight," she warned Emily, "and lean with the turn."

Clenching her jaw, Maggie picked up speed and weaved through the slowing vehicles. Traffic from West 68th Street drove through the intersection in one-way traffic.

There was no right turn, but that didn't stop Maggie.

She turned into the oncoming traffic, maneuvering the bike past a truck that almost collided right into them, and headed down the street amid the approaching cars.

The surviving pursuit vehicle tried to follow, but as it turned to tail them, the van Maggie had dodged hit the SUV side on and sent the car flipping onto its side and over onto its back.

Emily whooped and cheered, her braids whipping behind her in the wind. "You really are Jane Bond."

Maggie laughed and allowed a small cheer of her own, her heartwarming to the brave little girl holding on to her.

The elation didn't last long though. They may have lost the Russians for now, but one of the SUVs was still out there, and it was a long way to the British Consulate.

Chapter 10

Too long.

Traveling across town was out of the question. By now, the city would be teaming with undercover Russian operatives along with the more obvious ones they'd just escaped.

While Maggie preferred to work alone, she knew when things were tight. Getting Emily to the consulate alone was too big a risk and, as much as her ego hated to admit it, she needed help.

Snaking through the streets, taking alleyways when she could, Maggie headed for Ashton's apartment on West 59th Street. She stopped around the corner on 10th Avenue and ditched the bike behind a dumpster.

"What are you doing?" Maggie asked.

Emily fiddled with the notch of a container on the

back of the bike and opened the lid. "There's pizza in here. You don't let perfectly good pizza go to waste."

With two pizza boxes in hand, Maggie led Emily down the street and into the apartment building. As far as she could tell, no one spotted them. Right now, Aleksandar's crew would be scattered around the city, watching and waiting for them to turn up. Perhaps even staking out the British Consulate. Right now, they needed to lay low.

"Nice place," Emily said, surveying in the apartment. She slumped onto the couch and sniffed the pizza boxes. "Mind if I watch some TV?"

"Sure." Maggie checked through the peephole in the front door. Her muscles were stiff, the impact from her fight with Aleksandar settling in now they weren't racing through the city for dear life.

After some searching, Maggie found painkillers in the bathroom and washed off the blood from her face. Her reflection was paler than usual, and her hand tremored. It took a moment for her to register the odd feeling. Fear.

Maggie would be lying if she said she didn't get a thrill from her work. An adrenaline-fueled high coursed through her in the heat of the moment, when all she could focus on was staying alive and taking down whatever adversary stood in her way. Yes, fear was a familiar companion, but it was also exhilarating.

This fear felt different.

Then again, she'd never been on a mission like this. Or rather, *she'd* never been like *this* on a mission.

Raising her t-shirt, she stood to the side and appraised her tummy. She wasn't showing yet, but it was only a matter of weeks before the beginnings of a baby bump blossomed there. Nothing in her life would be the same, and whether she was ready for it or not, change was coming.

Ashton kept a first aid kit in his bedroom, and Maggie dug it out from the fitted wardrobes. Her phone lay on the bedside table. It was time to call in.

"Maggie." Danielle Hawkins answered on the first ring. "What's your status."

So much for hello.

"I have the witness. We're safe for now, but the situation is too volatile to reach you."

"Then we'll come to you. What's your location?"

Maggie gave Ashton's address.

"It might take a while to get a detail together. Stay inside until we get there."

Maggie bristled. Regardless of what Danielle seemed to think, this wasn't Maggie's first time in the field. The whole reason she was even involved was because Danielle and the rest of Jonathan Cole's team couldn't access the Russian Consulate. Maggie would like to see Danielle survive what Maggie had accomplished so far.

Hanging up without a goodbye, Maggie pocketed her phone and returned to Emily with the first aid kit.

"Who were you talking to?" Emily asked, chewing with her mouth open.

"Help." Maggie sat down beside her. "We'll wait here until they come for us."

Emily's shoulders relaxed. "Then I can see my parents?"

"I expect they'll be desperate to see you." Maggie opened the first aid kit. "Let me take a look at those knees."

Emily complied, taking another bite of her pepperoni and cheese slice while she flicked the TV channels to some cartoons. The abrasions were nothing to worry about, but they still needed cleaning. Dirt and small bits of rubble were stuck to the skin from her fall.

"This might sting a little," Maggie said, uncapping an antibacterial spray. She covered the wound with it and wiped the dirt off with a clean cloth.

Emily hissed, but she didn't complain or jerk away. Maggie smiled, liking the girl more and more. Not many kids Emily's age could go through what she had and still put on a brave face.

"That was quite the swing back there," noted Maggie, moving on to the next knee.

Emily gave a sheepish grin. "I'm on the little league team."

"I'm not surprised with a shot like that." Had it not been for Emily's attack, the whole mission could have ended down there in the subway. "You're very brave, Emily."

Emily ducked her head. "I don't feel brave."

Maggie tilted Emily's chin with her hand and met her eyes. "But you are."

"I ran away," she whispered.

"When?" Maggie asked, getting up and sitting next to Emily on the couch.

"When the man was attacked."

"What man?" Maggie probed. She still didn't know the name of the dead UN official, and Maggie hated missing information.

Emily shrugged. "I don't know. He was at the party. I needed the bathroom, and the one downstairs was being used, so I went upstairs. Only it's a big house, and I got lost. I went into the wrong room, and that's when I saw it."

Maggie leaned forward. "What did you see?"

Emily's bottom lip shook. "They stuck a needle into the man's neck, and he started shaking. Then he just stopped."

A needle. Danielle had said the means of the assassination were undetectable, which was why Emily was key to it all. Without her, the official's death could be passed off as a heart attack, or something similar. A shot of an untraceable substance into the bloodstream could induce cardiac arrest. It wouldn't be the first-time Maggie had come across the likes of it.

The Russians had covered their tracks. But they didn't count on Emily.

"I'm sorry you had to see that." Maggie wrapped her

arm over Emily's small shoulders. "Did you get a look at the attacker's face?"

Emily nodded. "I ran before they could get me, but the guy from the subway grabbed me when I got to the bottom of the stairs, and the next thing I knew, I woke up in the building with the Russians."

Aleksandar. He had been the one to take Emily away. Maggie was especially glad the little girl got the swing on him.

"Like I said, brave. And you're going to have to keep being brave." Emily was tough, and it would do her well for what lay ahead. Having to testify against a foreign government was the last thing a child should have to go through. Considering the magnitude of the crimes committed, Emily wouldn't be safe for a long time. At least not until she testified. Relations between Russia and the West were strained, and the Russians had already tried to remove Emily from the picture once.

"I'm scared," Emily whispered, her deep brown eyes glossy with tears.

Maggie gave her a squeeze and rubbed her arm. "That's okay. Being scared is part of being brave. What matters is that you keep going anyway, even if things seem bad. You're a fighter, and what do fighters do?"

Emily looked up at her. "Fight?"

"That's right." Maggie bumped her fist with Emily's. "We fight, and we keep on fighting."

Emily nodded, setting a determined jaw like she had done back inside the Russian Consulate. "I can do that."

"Good," said Maggie, closing the first aid kit and sinking into the sofa with Emily. "Now scoot over and quit hogging the pizza."

E mily regarded Maggie with an arched eyebrow. "You're out of your mind."

They'd been in the apartment for half an hour and were tucking in for a second helping of luke-warm pizza. Maggie's stomach rumbled in pleasure, having been neglected since the night before. She'd never been able to eat much before an assignment, especially one as important as hostage rescue.

"I'm telling you," Maggie replied, goading Emily, "I think Chicago's got the upper hand with the deep dish."

Not that it stopped her from delving into her third slice. It was greasy, laden with cheese and pepperoni, and the perfect comfort food after an afternoon of running for your life.

"Nope." Emily swiped the air with conviction. "It's New York slice or nothing at all."

Maggie shrugged and went in for another bite. The base was so thin that it dangled in front of her in a flopping mess and she had to maneuver her mouth down and around to catch it.

Emily giggled as she witnessed the spectacle. "Tourists. You're eating it all wrong."

Maggie put the slice down and sipped on some soda, kicking her boots off. "All right, smarty pants, show me the mystical ways of eating pizza."

"You fold it like this," Emily instructed, taking a new slice for herself and folding it, so both sides of the crust touched, creating a sturdier hold. "That way, the topping doesn't splat on the sidewalk." Emily laughed and pointed to Maggie's lap where a big glob of cheese had landed on her trousers. "Or on your jeans."

Maggie collected the cheese and ate it, sticking her tongue out at Emily. "Okay, I'll give you that, but deep dish is still better."

Emily sniggered and tuned back into her cartoons playing on Ashton's flat screen.

"What is this rubbish," Maggie asked, forgoing a napkin and licking her fingers.

"It's not rubbish," Emily said, eyes glued to a chubby little boy and his superhero sausage dog. "It's Tommy and Sir Barksalot."

"Cartoons have gone downhill since I was young," Maggie said, enjoying their little back and forth. Maggie wasn't much of a people person, but she liked Emily more than most adults she'd come across.

"Maybe," Emily countered, not missing a beat, "but at least we have color TVs now."

"I'm not that old," Maggie scoffed, taking another bite of folded pizza.

As she watched Emily laugh along to the cartoons, Maggie's mind turned to her pregnancy. Would she have a daughter? Would she be brave and resilient like Emily? She might even look a little like Emily, with her dark skin like Leon's and those big, beautiful eyes that didn't miss much.

The idea that a new life was forming inside her was surreal. A life that would grow into a child with their own personality, thoughts, and feelings. Would they be kind like Leon? Always considering how others are doing? Would they be resourceful and able to look after themselves like Maggie? Or would they be completely different, and grow up to be an artist or a scientist? She certainly hoped so. The further away their child was from her and Leon's type of work, the better.

There was an entire realm of possibilities inside of her. Possibilities that could change Maggie's life forever.

"So, Emily," Maggie said, interrupting her show as the superhero sausage dog saved the day, "what are you going to be when you grow up?"

"Hmm," Emily said, brow creased in thought.

"A baseball player?" Maggie suggested, topping Emily's glass up with soda. "I'm sure a team would be glad to have you with a swing like that."

Emily took a gulp of her soft drink and swirled the

glass like she was sipping on an aged Bordeaux. "I like sports, but I don't think I'd want to play professionally."

"What about a lawyer, like your mom?" Maggie asked certain Emily's mother held her wine glass the same way.

"I don't think so." Emily scrunched her nose. "She's super stressed all the time, and she thinks her boss is an assho— I mean, he's a jerk. I think I'd like to be an entrepreneur. That way, I'd get to be the boss, and no one can tell me what to do."

Maggie leaned over and held her glass to Emily. "I like your style."

"I like yours, too, Jane Bond," Emily said, clinking her glass with Maggie's. "You're kinda a badass."

The doorbell rang a while later. Maggie wiped the pizza grease off on her already dirty clothes and whipped out the baton to full length.

She crept to the front door, ready to attack, and checked the peephole. She sighed in relief when she saw Danielle standing impatiently with a detail of armed men. The cavalry had arrived.

Maggie swung open the door, and her allies ducked inside. They wore white jumpsuits, scattered in blobs of paint to masquerade as decorators, and carried cans of paint and a set of ladders.

"Thanks for coming," Maggie said, closing the door behind them before any of the neighbors got too nosey and noticed the host of people in the hallway.

"We have a van waiting in the underground garage to transport the witness," Danielle said.

"Maggie?" Emily called, coming to see who had arrived.

Emily stopped dead and eyed Danielle. The pizza box dropped from her hands and the entire apartment filled with her screams.

Chapter 11

Maggie ran to Emily and held her by the arms.

"Emily, what is it? What's wrong?"

Emily stabbed a finger at Danielle. "It was her. She was the one who killed that guy."

Maggie straightened and stepped between Danielle and Emily. Her mind raced to catch up, to figure out what was happening.

"It was her," Emily cried again. "She's with the British government, I heard her tell my mom at the party. She said she worked here in New York."

Danielle's crew lunged forward, shoving Maggie out of the way. Before she could retaliate, one of them snuck behind Emily and jabbed a needle into her neck.

Emily blinked a few times, her face a map of confusion before she slumped forward. Maggie lunged and caught her before she fell, holding the unconscious little girl in her arms.

"What was in that?" Maggie demanded.

"Relax," Danielle said. "It's a sedative."

Maggie lay Emily on the floor and sprung to her feet. In two strides, she grabbed Danielle by the shoulders and pinned her to the nearest wall so hard the framed picture hanging there fell to the wooden floor. "Why the fuck are you drugging her?"

Danielle's men reached for their concealed weapons.

"It's okay, boys," Danielle assured, before turning back to Maggie. "She was hysterical. We can't exactly take her down to the van kicking and screaming."

Hysterical. There was that word again.

Maggie released her hold of Danielle and backed away. "Is what she said true? Were you the one she saw kill the UN official?"

"Yes," Danielle admitted, straightening her suit, the only one of the detail not wearing overalls.

Maggie glared at the woman, curling her hands into fists. "Which UN official?"

"Dimitri Udinov."

"The Russian ambassador?" The final puzzle piece clicked into place. Fury burned in Maggie's veins. "You tricked me. You let me believe the Russian's had killed a British official, but it was the other way around."

The woman frowned. "I don't remember telling you anything of the sort. We refrained from telling you the full story in case you were compromised, as you pointed out in our first meeting."

Danielle and Jonathan Cole hadn't told any lies, which explained why Maggie hadn't suspected the deception. Emily was indeed a witness. What they failed to mention was that she was a witness to a British operation.

Maggie inched closer to Emily, her chest rising and falling in a chemically induced slumber. "Why did our government want Udinov dead?"

"He was spotted in multiple meetings with former KGB affiliates," Danielle said. "Our undercover intelligence reported plans to assassinate select world leaders at the next UN summit, including the Prime Minister."

"And the Americans were in on this, too?" Maggie guessed. They had to be to allow the operation to take place on their turf.

"The President was one of their proposed targets, too," Danielle confirmed.

Maggie counted six men in Danielle's detail. "And the Russians were holding Emily as proof against us?"

Us. The affiliation tasted like ash in her mouth.

Danielle's lips thinned. "They got to the girl before I could. We have reason to believe that was their intention. Thanks to you, now they won't be able to."

Aleksandar had grabbed Emily, but he never meant to kill her. He wanted to protect her. Protect her from the very people Maggie worked for.

Thinking back on it, the Russians had plenty of

opportunities to shoot Emily dead. In Central Park. On the Subway. Even during the chase through the streets, one of them could have leaned out the SUV and pulled the trigger. Maggie hadn't considered it at the time, too busy trying to escape and stay alive, but there it was. They didn't take the shot because they wanted Emily alive.

Seven sets of eyes stayed on her, and Maggie considered her odds at taking them all out. "Why kill Udinov if you had proof of his plans?" she asked Danielle, trying to understand. "You could have outed him publicly."

"It was a matter of national security." A coy smile played at the woman's lips. "I'm sure you understand."

Maggie laughed, but it was bitter and burning with rage. "You didn't have sufficient evidence to prove his plans, did you?" Or at least, no proof the British government could use. Not if they attained it through illegal means.

"His plot was a legitimate threat," Danielle said, voice sharpening. "Now it isn't."

Maggie couldn't bring herself to care about any of it. All she cared about was Emily's fate. "Where are you taking her?"

Danielle raised her chin. "The situation must be contained."

"Contained?" Maggie closed her eyes. She knew what it meant.

"We can't afford any loose ends."

"Her name is Emily Wallace," Maggie said through gritted teeth. "She's twelve years old."

"A pity," Danielle said, loftily, "but collateral damage is unavoidable sometimes."

Maggie balled her fists so hard her knuckles cracked. "It's entirely avoidable if you're even remotely competent at your job. What kind of assassin gets caught by a child?"

Danielle crossed her arms. "I regret what happened, believe me, I do. But our hands are tied."

Maggie's mind raced for a solution. For anything that could save Emily. "There must be another way. A way that doesn't involve killing a little girl."

Danielle waved a hand at Emily sprawled on the floor. "You heard her. I was a guest at the party representing the consulate, and she witnessed me killing Udinov. She knows too much." Danielle stated, her words hard and unyielding. "The decision has already been made."

With Emily able to connect Danielle to Britain, it linked the government directly to the murder of Udinov. Emily was a risk they couldn't afford, no matter how deplorable it was to eliminate her.

"You're just going to kill an innocent child?" Maggie searched each of her colleagues faces, making sure to stare each of them in the eye.

She was met with blank stares.

"Why not have me do it back at the consulate?" Maggie asked, her blood boiling. The tremor from before was back, but it wasn't fear for herself or the life growing inside her this time. "Why have me break Emily out and keep her alive if you're just going to kill her anyway?"

"We need to question her," Danielle said. "Find out what the Russians already know and what they gleaned from her before you arrived."

Bile rose in Maggie's throat. "Interrogation first, then death."

"It will be quick and humane," Danielle assured, like a vet telling a bereaved owner their pet was going to be put down. "A doctor will administer a lethal injection tonight. It will feel like she's falling asleep."

"You can't do this," Maggie yelled, stepping forwards.

"Stand down," Danielle ordered like she could ever be Maggie's superior.

In a wave of fury, Maggie swung at Danielle, but her men held Maggie back.

Danielle clicked her fingers, and one of the men hoisted Emily's small frame over one shoulder. She stopped at the door and turned back to Maggie. "You did well, Agent. The Consul-General expects an in-person report tomorrow morning before you leave. We'll take things from here."

And just like that, Danielle and the man carrying Emily left the apartment, followed by the rest of her team.

Maggie fell to her knees as the door slammed closed.

Chapter 12

Maggie brought up the final bites of pizza and spat out a mouthful of bile that burned her throat on the way up.

Emily.

Maggie stood and rinsed out her mouth, splashing her clammy face with water. Her mind swam, trying to come to terms with what had happened. Right now, unconscious and alone, Emily was in the back of Danielle's van, being transported to a secure location.

Maggie's nails dug into her palms as she bit back tears.

Unknowingly or not, she had delivered Emily to her death.

She told Emily she would get her back to her parents. She promised to keep her safe.

Her fingers itched to wreck the place. To smash, and tear, and break everything in sight. Maggie paced the apartment, her thoughts racing. She completed the mission given to her, just as she always did. Did what was asked of her, even with the seemingly impossible odds.

Maggie had done plenty of things for Queen and country she wasn't proud of. Things that kept her awake at night. Things that haunted her dreams. Things she could never take back. The weight of it took a toll on her. A toll she gladly paid to do what must be done. To do what others could not.

The one thing that kept her going that allowed her to do those things was the knowledge that it was all for the greater good. Until now, she'd never felt like the enemy.

But what could she have done? Fought Danielle? Stopped them from taking Emily?

It wasn't Danielle she would be defying. It wasn't her boss Jonathan Cole or even the entire consulate.

Maggie would be defying her country.

She was guilty of a whole list of crimes, but treason wasn't one of them.

Maggie collapsed onto the couch and ran a hand through her hair. The cushions were still warm from where Emily sat eating pizza, the noise of cartoons still played in the background. The weight of it bore down on her, threatening to suffocate her with tears. Maggie had taken many lives over the years, but never a child's. Most of the people she took out had done despicable things. Deplorable things. They deserved what came to them.

Not Emily.

Not a twelve-year-old girl who stumbled into the wrong place and the wrong time.

A set of tears slipped from her eyes and tracked down her face. Maggie wiped them away with an angry fist. She didn't get to sit around and cry or feel sorry for herself. Not after what she let happen. Not now, knowing what was going to happen to Emily before the night was over. Maggie may not be the one administering the lethal injection, but she might as well be. Danielle never would have retrieved Emily without Maggie's help.

Maggie worried at her nail, a habit she had gotten rid of back in training as a teenager. The whole situation was unraveling her.

Jonathan Cole and Danielle hadn't been exaggerating when they told Maggie her operation was of the highest priority for the sake of national security.

If the Russians had managed to use Emily as they planned, if she'd testified about what she saw and helped prove Britain was responsible, there was no telling the extent of the damage caused.

Relations between Russia and the UK and US were already tense. It was a delicate balance, and even the slightest thing could tip the scale, never mind something as damning as murder. If anyone caught wind of the assassination—especially during a UN party—all hell would break loose.

It would rip open Pandora's box, and the threat of war would be very, very real.

The testimony of a twelve-year-old girl could result in World War III. It was far too big a risk.

Not that it made things easier. Not that it made Maggie feel any better.

Intellectually and strategically, Emily Wallace couldn't be allowed to live.

But morally? Emotionally?

Maggie got up and paced the apartment again.

Nothing she could say would change the minds of her superiors. Bishop wasn't even privy to the mission. The Director-General would know, of course, but she was the one who had Bishop send Maggie to New York in the first place.

Even Danielle was following orders given to her by Jonathan Cole, which would have been passed down from higher up, too. Something, as classified as this, would run all the way up the food chain. This was top level stuff, and there was no way any of them would discuss a change of plan with her.

Maggie stopped in the middle of the room and bit her lip as the idea crossed her mind.

No, she couldn't.

Her heart thumped in her chest. It was insane. Not to mention dangerous. She looked over her shoulder to where Emily had sat, a hand over her stomach. Maggie couldn't say anything that would help Emily.

But she could *do* something.

She had two phone calls to make. Maggie dialed the number before she changed her mind.

"Mags."

"Ashton, I need your help."

Chapter 13

What am I doing?

The question circled for the hundredth time since she'd made up her mind. It was the bracelet that sparked this insane idea of hers. Maggie had secured it around Emily's wrist back inside the consulate, but she never thought she'd use it for this.

The tracking device concealed inside the bracelet showed Emily's current location in Downtown Brooklyn.

Maggie, along with a team of Ashton's New York City contacts, crossed the Manhattan Bridge. Night had fallen, and the city lit up like a constellation of stars, the Empire State Building rising into the sky, a beacon of brilliant light. The cloak of darkness gave Maggie and her cohorts some much-needed cover, but it also meant Emily was running out of time.

Danielle said a doctor would arrive that night to kill Emily by lethal injection. A fate that only the worst of America's criminals received. At least in some states. Emily was about as far from being a criminal as a person could get, and Maggie refused to sit back and let her life be cut short because of Danielle's incompetence.

"Thank you for helping me," Maggie said to the driver, who seemed like the leader of the small crew.

The gruff man, who refused to tell Maggie his name, chewed on his cigar and blew out a puff of smoke. "I'm only doing this because I owe Ashton a favor."

Maggie hadn't asked Ashton many questions about the ragtag group he assembled for her. If he trusted them, that was enough for her. Even if most of them operated on the other side of the law.

Ashton hadn't revealed any confidential information to his contacts, but from the looks of their faces in the back of the van, they knew enough to know things were about to get dangerous.

None of them were happy about Maggie's no gun policy. She may be willing to defy her country and colleagues, but that didn't mean she wanted any of them dead. Murder was strictly off the table, at least on their end.

The heavens opened, and rain battered against the windshield of the van. Above, the gray clouds blotted out the full moon. A superstitious person might consider a night like this to be a bad omen.

Good thing Maggie wasn't superstitious.

The baton she'd stolen earlier lay across her lap, and she gripped it with her gloved hands, focusing on her breathing. On what she was about to do.

Maggie didn't make a habit of committing treason. Her work required a variety of illegal acts, but treason was a line she never wanted to cross. One she'd never even considered.

Until now.

A quirk of a smile settled on Maggie's lips. Her actions could only be considered treason if she got caught, and she had no intentions of letting that happen.

There were six mercenaries in the back of the van: three women, three men. Including Maggie and the driver, that made them a team of eight. Danielle would have more guards at her disposal, but Ashton assured Maggie each of his contacts was worth two normal agents. She only hoped he was right.

They exited the bridge and headed to the New York Naval Shipyard. The NYNS was decommissioned in the sixties and had since reinvented itself as commercial property. It catered to a wide scope of industries, from farming and manufacturing to entertainment, and was home to the largest set of production studios outside of Los Angeles.

Emily's tracker placed her inside an abandoned warehouse at the edge of the yard that looked out into the East River from Wallabout Bay.

Maggie's phone buzzed in her pocket.

"Do you have everything you need?" Maggie asked, forgoing hellos.

"Yes."

"Good. Meet me at pier K in one hour. Don't be late." Maggie hung up and turned off the phone. She'd done all she could.

Her driver approached one of the yard's entrance gates and spoke briefly with the guy manning it. From the tone, Maggie assumed they knew each other. The driver passed the man a thick fold of bills before continuing inside.

"Let's abandon the van here," Maggie said, scanning the docks. "I want the advantage of surprise."

Danielle's crew would still be on high alert. Until the witness was silenced, the Russians looking for her would continue to be a concern.

If Maggie's plan worked, none of them would see Emily Wallace ever again.

Ashton's band of mercenaries got out the van in silence, each dressed head to toe in black. Maggie pulled the balaclava over her head, making sure to conceal her hair, and secured a pair of night vision goggles over her eyes. Concealing her identity was vital, especially tonight.

Motioning for her team to follow, Maggie led her temporary troops into the rain-soaked night and approached the abandoned warehouse.

Wind whistled across the bay and sent shivers down Maggie's spine, stinging like iced fingers clawing at her skin. The night air was warm, but still, Maggie's teeth chattered. Clamping her jaw, she pressed forward until they reached the entrance of the warehouse.

The crew split into prearranged groups, leaving Maggie on her own—just the way she liked it—and they slunk into position like phantoms in the night.

Waiting for the driver's signal, Maggie leaned down on her knees and hid between a rough outcrop of bushes and tall grass. Through her goggles, the world was shades of green. Two of Danielle's agents made rounds of the perimeter, guns in hands and eyes watchful.

Not watchful enough.

The driver and his partner aimed their dart guns at the agents from their spots behind a SUV. Their accuracy was impressive, even to Maggie. Thin darts struck both guards in the thigh, the dark tips protruding from their flesh long enough for them to realize their mistake.

A second pair of Ashton's mercenaries appeared from the darkness and caught the agents before they could fall with unceremonious thumps. The pair dragged the unconscious guards to the side of the building to sleep it off, while the rest of the mercenaries narrowed in from all angles and surrounded the building.

Maggie waited until the first pair breached the entrance and set off their smoke bomb before moving. Most of the windows were boarded and hid what lay within. Emily could be anywhere.

Yelling and gunshots echoed inside the cavernous

building, the whipping wind drawing the sounds outside to Maggie.

Circumventing the entrance, Maggie sprinted to the back of the warehouse. Like the front of the building, the windows at the back were boarded, too. Using her baton, Maggie wedged the weapon between the wood and the window frame and yanked it with all her strength.

The nails slid out without much fuss, the damp wood rotten with age and exposure.

Maggie risked a look inside to make sure the coast was clear. The familiar grunts of fighting reverberated through the bare brick walls, but the coast was clear. Sliding in, Maggie closed the wood back over the window as best she could and scanned her surroundings.

A two-story warehouse, Maggie found herself in a hallway at the foot of a set of stairs. The floor above was silent. She fiddled with her goggles and listened, the whole place pitch black thanks to one of her team dismantling the breaker and cutting the lights.

The floorboards creaked behind her. Maggie lashed out with her baton. The assailant dodged the attack and came in with one of his own. Maggie took the blow, a meaty fist striking her in the shoulder. Her arm rang with pain, but she held on to her baton and parried a right hook with it. As much as she would like to stand toe to toe with the big brute and let off some steam, Maggie had a job to do and didn't have time for distractions.

She and the brute circled in the little hallway, squaring

each other up. The agent didn't seem impressed with what he saw, but Maggie was used to that.

The man quirked a grin and lunged forward like a rugby player, going in for a takedown. Maggie twirled on the balls of her feet and spun, bringing the baton down like a whip, and bludgeoned the agent in the back of the head.

It had worked for her and Emily in the subway, and it worked for Maggie now. The agent fell to the floor and never got back up.

Maggie kicked him to make sure he was out, going over the options in her head. The fighting still raged on beyond the set of doors to her left, where Ashton's contacts were hopefully gaining the advantage.

Strategically, Danielle wouldn't place Emily anywhere near the entrance. She'd want her witness-turned-hostage as far away as possible. Somewhere they could keep her while they contained the breach.

That didn't leave many options, and Maggie ascended the steps on light feet, holding her baton close.

The top floor wasn't as big as the lower level. From what Maggie could tell, it took up a fraction of the space, and she passed two small offices as she crept down the hallway. Mold-covered carpet lined the floor, squishy under her feet and spotted with frayed holes and dark stains. A rat scurried away from Maggie, but she didn't squirm. She had bigger vermin to take care of tonight.

Only one more door remained. Unlike the others, it was closed, and a moving light shone under it.

Counting down from three, Maggie took a deep breath and rushed the door. Leaping into the air, Maggie kicked the wood, and it flew open, breaking from its rusted hinges. It was a foreman's room, larger than the other two offices with a wide, one-hundred-and-eighty-degree window that overlooked the shop floor and the fighting going on below.

Maggie's heart leapt as she spotted Emily on the office table.

But she wasn't alone.

A man fumbled with a flashlight and aimed it at Maggie. In his free hand, he held a needle filled with a clear substance. A vicious rage bubbled inside of Maggie. If the agent downstairs had slowed her even a moment more, she would have been too late. She would have committed treason with nothing to show for it.

Liquid spurted from the end of the needle as the doctor dropped the flashlight and made for Emily on the table.

Maggie raced over the fallen door and yanked the man back by the scruff of his shirt. Taking her baton in both hands, she scooped it over the doctor's head and caught him by the neck, pressing the weapon against his windpipe.

The doctor wriggled in her grasp, but his attempts to break free only made the process quicker, expelling his oxygen until it became too much for his body. Maggie held on tight as he slipped into unconsciousness and his eyes rolled to the back of his head. She let the doctor slip under her arms and splay out on the ground.

"Sorry, Doctor, but your services will not be needed tonight."

Maggie didn't check on him. The doctor would live. Instead, she went to the table where Emily lay.

Maggie's heart stopped as she got close.

Emily's eyes were closed. She wasn't moving.

Chapter 14

Maggie tapped Emily's face as panic welled inside her. Was she too late? Had the doctor already administered a dose of something else? Something lethal?

"Emily. Emily wake up."

Emily didn't move.

"Emily," Maggie said again, louder this time.

Nothing.

Slipping off one of her gloves, Maggie placed the back of her hand above Emily's lips and held her breath. Waited until—

There. Shallow but there all the same. Emily was breathing. She was still alive.

Digging into her pockets, Maggie brought out a small vial and unscrewed the cap. She placed the smelling salts under Emily's nose and waited.

Emily's eyes shot open, and her body jerked away from the smell. Maggie secured her by the shoulders as she came to, her clouded brain trying to catch up with where she was. They must have drugged her again after questioning.

Bastards. "It's me," Maggie whispered, wiping Emily's clammy face free from her braids. "Can you sit up?"

Emily groaned as Maggie hoisted her into a sitting position, holding a hand to her head. Maggie knew the feeling. Emily was in for a killer headache.

"Do you think you can walk?" They couldn't hang around any longer than necessary.

Emily's eyes widened, peering over Maggie's shoulder. "Watch out!"

Maggie spun in time to see Danielle striding towards her from the hallway. Maggie shoved Emily back and stood her ground, ready to face the woman whose botched mission caused all of this.

"Come on!" Maggie yelled in fluent Russian, springing forward to meet Danielle.

The women clashed in a collision of fists and anger.

Maggie evaded a kick aimed at her stomach and thrashed out with her baton. Danielle leaned back to dodge the swing, but it clipped her on the nose, and she reeled back, swearing as blood oozed from her nostrils.

"You not take her," Danielle rasped, her Russian flawed and rudimentary. She charged Maggie again, slapping her in the face with an open palm.

The blow caught Maggie off guard, and Danielle used the distraction to swipe her leg under Maggie's ankles and send her to the ground.

Maggie careened back and slammed into the floor. The baton slipped from her hands and rolled out of sight.

The fall was awkward and knocked the air from Maggie's lungs. Before she had time to suck in a breath, Danielle was on her. The agent kneeled, using her momentum to put power into the fist heading right for Maggie's face.

Maggie rolled to the side just in time, Danielle's fist smacking against the moldy carpet. Both women rushed to their feet, and Maggie felt a twinge of unease. Their speed was evenly matched.

"Bitch," Maggie swore, her voice pitched low and gruff to conceal her identity. Danielle was expecting Russians, and that's what Maggie gave her.

With a cry, Danielle shot forward again and lashed out with a foray of jabs. Maggie took the brunt of them, each one sorer than the last as Danielle built momentum.

Despite her mishap with the assassination, Danielle was good. More than good.

But Maggie was better.

Not that she was going to give away that secret, not just yet. She let Danielle believe she was gaining the upper hand, stumbling backward, inching closer and closer to the foot of the stairs at the end of the hallway. Danielle twisted her hips and raised her leg into a kick.

Spotting the perfect opportunity, Maggie moved in sync with the other agent, her perfect mirror, and scooped Danielle's leg into her arm. Maggie pinned Danielle in a death grip and reached for the collar of her jacket, pulling her forwards.

With her leg pinned, Danielle had to focus all her attention on staying upright. Maggie pivoted and shoved Danielle. Hard.

Danielle yelped as her first step yielded nothing but air, and she tumbled down the stairs, hitting every step and collapsing in a crumbled mess of limbs at the bottom landing. Maggie assessed her from her position at the top. A few broken ribs, maybe a fractured bone here or there in her arms and legs. Nothing that wouldn't heal in time.

Certain Danielle wasn't getting back up, Maggie ignored the guilty rumblings in her stomach and returned to the office.

"Maggie?" Emily asked, uncertain.

Maggie took off her balaclava and knelt by the table Emily was using to keep herself standing. "It's me. Are you okay?"

"I think so," Emily said, her voice sluggish from the drugs. "Are you?"

The fighting had ceased on the workshop floor. Maggie peered out the window and found Ashton's contacts binding the wrists of the fallen agents with plastic zip ties. That would keep them busy once they came to.

"I've had worse," Maggie said, holding Emily by the

waist and wrapping the girl's arm over her shoulder. "Now come on, let's get you out of here."

The agents may be down, but Maggie and Emily weren't out of hot water just yet.

Chapter 15

Maggie said her farewells to the nameless driver and the rest of Ashton's contacts. They fought well and refrained from killing anyone like she'd asked, but Maggie would see the final part of her mission through alone. The less people who knew, the better.

The van drove off, wheels crunching on gravel as it exited the old shipyard, leaving Maggie and Emily in the pouring rain. The sky rumbled, the waves beyond the bay crashing amid a coming storm.

"Why aren't we going with them?" Emily asked, teeth chattering.

Maggie took off her jacket and wrapped it around Emily's shoulders. "We have somewhere else to be."

It wasn't too far from the warehouse, but it took longer

than Maggie liked, thanks to sedatives still coursing through Emily's veins.

They arrived at pier K with minutes to spare, and Maggie's racing pulse relaxed once she spotted the vessel tethered and waiting for them. The captain of the RBS-11 was an ex-marine and a current member of the US Coast Guard. His face matched the photo Ashton sent along earlier that night for confirmation, a stern looking man with a weatherworn face and a thicket of salt and pepper hair. If anyone could get the Wallaces out of the city, it was him.

A woman in a dark trench coat spotted Maggie and Emily walking up the pier and ran to them.

Emily was a young clone of her mother, a beautiful woman in her forties with high cheekbones and a regal air to her movements. She collected Emily in her arms and cried a wail into the wind

"My baby."

"Mom," said Emily, closing her eyes and snuggling into her mother's embrace.

Ms. Wallace looked up to Maggie with glistening eyes. "You did it."

Maggie cleared her throat and gathered herself together. "I promised your daughter I would keep her safe."

Mr. Wallace arrived close behind his wife and lifted Emily into his arms for a fierce hug.

"Thank you," he said, unable to say anything more.

"If there is anything we can do," said Ms. Wallace, shaking Maggie's hand, "Anything you need, just say the word."

Maggie looked both of Emily's parents in the eye. It was important they listened to her.

"I need you to follow through with the plans we discussed. Don't try to contact anyone you know. No relatives, no friends, and especially not anyone from work. Your old life is over, and if you want to make sure your daughter sees her next birthday, you must accept that."

The British, the Americans, and the Russians would all be searching for Emily. A key witness like her could not be allowed to disappear. They all needed her for their own reasons, and none of them would stop looking for her. Not for a long time.

Ms. Wallace nodded, her face serious. "It's a small price to pay to have our daughter back." Without warning, she wrapped her arms tight around Maggie, her rose scented perfume tickling her nose.

"Keep her safe," Maggie whispered. She had done all she could. It was up to them now.

"We will."

"And remember," Maggie said, staring Ms. Wallace in the eyes, "if you go public about the assassination, not only will you endanger Emily's life, but the lives of millions of people. You know the kind of people involved in all of this. It won't end well."

"I know what's at risk," Ms. Wallace assured her stern

expression a mirror image of her daughter's. "And not only for my family. I understand why this truth must be buried."

Maggie believed her. She had to if she was going to follow through with her plan.

Mr. Wallace was by their side now, and Emily was back on her feet, still a little unsteady. The effects would wear off soon. All she needed was something to eat and a good night's rest.

Maggie released herself gently from Ms. Wallace's hold, all of them sodden in the rain. "All right, you better get going."

Emily stepped forward. "Thank you, Maggie."

A warmth spread over Maggie, and the urge to burst into tears sprung behind her eyes. She willed them back and leaned into the brave little girl who would soon be a young woman.

Emily peered over at the boat. "Where are we going?"

"Away," said Maggie, tugging her jacket closer around Emily. She needed to stay warm. "It's not safe for you here anymore."

"Are you coming with us?" Emily asked with innocent, hopeful eyes.

"No, but you'll be safe. I promise." Ashton wouldn't let Maggie down.

"Will I see you again?"

Maggie smiled. "Perhaps one day."

Emily stared down at her feet. "Can I call you once we get there?"

"It's best if I don't know where you are." If her colleagues or the Russians learned of Maggie's escapades, they'd torture everything they could out of her, but Maggie couldn't reveal a location she didn't know. She spoke to them all, trying but failing to keep the emotion from spilling into her voice. "Once you're safe, you'll be taken to a private airport. A plane is already waiting for you."

"What about passports?" Ms. Wallace asked, clutching her husband's hand. "Money?"

"It's all covered," Maggie assured. "A friend has arranged everything you'll need."

The Wallaces would soon have new names, taking on aliases like Maggie had done countless times before. It would be difficult for them at first, but they'd get used to it. They had to.

"And you trust this friend?" Mr. Wallace asked.

"With my life," said Maggie. And with theirs. Ashton had really come through for her on this one.

Emily hugged Maggie. "Goodbye, Jane Bond."

"Goodbye, brave girl," Maggie said, allowing a tear to fall and get lost amid the rain. She straightened up and held out a fist. "Remember, what do fighters do?"

Emily grinned and bumped her knuckles against Maggie's. "We keep on fighting."

Maggie stayed by the pier as the Wallaces boarded their boat. The engine rumbled to life, and they zoomed across the East River until it disappeared in a blanket of darkness. Life was full of gray areas, and while she may have defied her government, she did not fail Emily Wallace.

Some things in life were more important than following orders. Even though she'd gone against her country's wishes, she had still eliminated any threat of war between the nations. While things didn't go as planned, the sole witness to Udinov's murder was gone. By the time the night was over, Emily Wallace would have vanished, never to be seen or heard from again. Her parents and the strings Ashton pulled would see to that.

Maggie didn't make a habit of placing her trust in others, but she put her faith in a mother and father's love. Without Emily, the Russians couldn't prove anything, and Danielle and her team were in the clear. Any threat caused by the chain of events had been removed, and Maggie pulled it off without ending the life of an innocent.

Resolute in her decision, Maggie left the shipyard and slipped into the shadows of the night.

Chapter 16

22 SEPTEMBER

Maggie sat with folded arms across from Jonathan Cole the next morning.

"If this is a joke," she said, "I don't find it funny."

"I can assure you, this is far from a joke." Jonathan bristled and fidgeted in his chair. From the wrinkles in his untucked shirt and the bags under his eyes, the Consul-General didn't get much sleep last night.

As for Maggie, she slept like a baby once she fell into Ashton's king-sized bed. Her friend had called an hour ago to let Maggie know the Wallaces were safe and had made their way out of the US undetected.

Jonathan's assistant sat to his left, scribbling notes and keeping his head down, doing what he could to blend into the background and avoid his boss's wrath. Mr. Cole was like a bear with a sore arse, and that was before he spilled his coffee down himself.

Maggie turned her attention to Danielle, sitting to Jonathan's right. The day before hadn't left Maggie unscathed. Her muscles ached, and her skin was covered with several cuts and bruises, but it was nothing she couldn't hide under a long-sleeve shirt and some makeup.

Danielle didn't fare as well. Arm in a sling, she sat scowling in another bland suit, the one from the night before well and truly ruined. The best dry cleaner in New York City couldn't have removed the blood and dirt from that ensemble.

One of her eyes was bloodshot and surrounded by a ghastly purple bruise that ran all the way across to her broken nose. Danielle winced as she coughed, her ribs likely wrapped up tight under her blouse, and left to heal on their own. If Maggie felt any remorse at causing Danielle pain, it was tampered by the satisfaction that she'd rescued Emily without outing herself as a traitor.

"You lost the witness again," Maggie spat, putting on a show for her colleagues. She slammed her fist down on the desk and tea sloshed from her cup. "After everything, I went through to get Emily Wallace to you, you managed to lose her in less than ten hours."

"We were ambushed by the Russians," Danielle said. "They outnumbered us three to one."

Maggie raised an eyebrow. She wasn't the only one adding some flair to the real story. Then again, Danielle's pride wouldn't allow her to admit she had been bested by a detail half her size.

Jonathan mopped his head with a handkerchief and wrung his hands. "The situation is unfortunate."

"Unfortunate?" Maggie interrupted, waving her hands in exasperation. "What kind of half-baked operation are you running here?"

"I will remind you, Ms. Black, that you are not the authority here. You do not get to question me or my operatives."

Maggie balked at that and leaned forward. "Fine, but you can rest assured that Director-General Helmsley will hear all I have to say about the shocking levels of incompetence from this office."

Letting her words settle, Maggie kicked her chair back and shrugged on her jacket.

"Where do you think you're going?" Jonathan demanded.

Maggie stopped by the door with a hand on the handle. "You're on your own with this one. I did what I was sent here to do, and I don't intend to board your sinking ship."

"You can't leave," Jonathan spluttered. "You haven't given your full report yet."

Opening the door, Maggie glanced over her shoulder. "I'll give it straight to the Director- General herself. Besides, you don't have time to sit around asking me questions. I suggest you use what time you have left to prepare for your own debriefing."

Without another word, she walked out of Jonathan Cole's office and slammed the door. Her work there was done, and it was time to go home.

Chapter 17

Maggie arrived at the health center five minutes early. It was a crisp October Saturday, and she had wrapped up warm for the short walk across the Thames from her apartment.

"Hi, my name's Maggie Black. I have a follow-up appointment with Dr. Kahn."

The receptionist told her to take a seat, and Maggie joined the little cluster of women. The woman in the seat next to her looked like her water could break at any moment.

"You have this to look forward to," she huffed at Maggie, pointing to her swollen ankles and feet. Maggie tried to imagine her stomach that big. Stretch pants were definitely in her future. She couldn't wait.

A lot of things in her life were about to change.

Leaving the Unit was the biggest. Maggie had spent the last eleven years building her career and working non-stop, hopping from one country to the next. It was a dangerous and thrilling lifestyle. A lifestyle she could no longer live.

Though she'd miss parts of her old life, motherhood was her assignment now and, like every mission, she completed before, she'd give it her all. Failing this job wasn't an option.

Ms. Wallace walked away from her career as an international human rights lawyer in a heartbeat for Emily. Maggie now understood why.

Working for the Unit wasn't like most careers. Plenty of women returned to work after having a baby, more than capable of juggling a career and motherhood, both full-time jobs in their own right.

But Maggie couldn't do both. She couldn't be there for a morning routine or spend afternoons in the park with her child if she was in a foreign country taking out bad guys. She couldn't return home from the office in time to collect her child from school. To make dinner, or kiss her little one goodnight.

Half the time, Maggie couldn't even tell anyone where

she was. It wasn't fair to do that to a child. To only be there between missions, not knowing if she'd ever make it back to see their sweet little face again.

Agents weren't known for long life expectancies.

Even her own mother died before her time, the car crash stealing her away from Maggie when she was just six years old. She knew what it was liking losing her mum, and she refused to let her child suffer the same fate.

If that meant walking away from the Unit, then so be it.

"What are you having," Maggie asked the heavily pregnant woman beside her.

"I don't know," she replied, pleasant and warm despite her clear discomfort. "We want it to be a surprise."

We.

Rummaging in her purse, Maggie found her phone and called Leon again. Bishop said he should be getting back from an assignment today, and she couldn't wait any longer to tell him. She wasn't sure how he'd take the news, but he needed to know. She wanted him to be the first person she told.

The voicemail picked up. He must not be back yet.

"Hi, it's me. I heard you'd be back today. I know we haven't spoken much since Venice, but I'd like to see you. I have something to tell you, and it's not the kind of thing you say over the phone. Anyway, ring me back once you get this."

Maggie hung up as the doctor called her name. She

tucked her phone away and followed Dr. Kahn into his office.

"Nice to see you again, Maggie. How have you been?"

"Great, thanks," she said, taking off her scarf and coat.

Keeping the baby turned out to be an easier decision that she expected. After New York, only one route felt right. While she didn't think badly of those who chose to terminate their pregnancy, it wasn't an option she could personally come to terms with.

Putting her child up for adoption was out of the question, too. Maggie knew firsthand how the system affected a child, and she wouldn't put someone through that if she could help it. In many ways, Maggie wouldn't have ended up in the Unit if she had a loving family and decent upbringing.

Dark thoughts surfaced from the recesses of her mind, taking her back to the night she first killed someone at the tender age of fifteen. Memories tried to push forward to remind her what led to that moment, to show her the domino effect it had on her life ever since.

Maggie forced the thoughts down and focused on the present. Focused on Dr. Kahn and her new future.

"We got the results back from your hCG blood test." Dr. Kahn straightened the tissue box on his desk like he thought she might have need of them soon. *Why would she need tissues?* And then, seeming to realize what he was doing, he folded his hands on top of the file with her medical records.

Maggie sat up in her chair. A knot tightened in her stomach, her heart fluttering like a scared bird. "And?"

Dr. Kahn stared at the file instead of looking her in the eye. "I'm afraid I have some bad news."

"What?" Maggie's fists clenched, but this wasn't a battle she could win with violence. She forced herself to stay seated. "Is everything okay with the baby?"

Dr. Kahn sighed and finally looked up. The pull of his brow and the supposedly comforting smile on his lips reminded Maggie of the doctors on TV when they delivered terrible news. "Ms. Black, I'm sorry to say, but you are no longer pregnant. You've had a miscarriage."

"What?" Maggie blinked, her mind struggling to catch up to his words, to understand the full weight of his implications. *Miscarriage.* Fear, piercing and acidic, sent her heart racing. "Was it because of me?" she asked, her voice rising. Breaking. "Was it something I did?"

The fighting. Risking her life to save Emily Wallace. Had all that killed her unborn baby? Things had been fine when Dr. Kahn saw her last week, aside from some light bleeding. He said it was normal. That he needed to run some simple tests.

"No, no," Dr. Kahn said quickly, shaking his head. "Nothing like that. There were some chromosomal abnormalities that caused problems with the fetus's development."

The fetus.

Maggie covered her mouth with a shaking hand,

holding back the urge to be sick. "You promise me," she wailed, hating the pleading, broken one in her voice. "Promise this wasn't my fault."

"I promise you," Dr. Kahn assured, offering her a sad smile. "There's nothing you could have done. These things are unfortunately common in the first trimester."

A flush of relief spread through Maggie, but it fled just as quickly, shame filling the empty space in her heart. It didn't change anything. She had still lost her baby.

The life growing inside her wasn't there anymore.

Like it had never been there at all. Except that is was. Her whole life was going to change. *Everything* was going to be different. And now, that hope—that joy—was gone.

"I know the news can come as a shock. Is there anyone I can call?"

"No," Maggie heard herself say, but it was like she was somewhere else. Gone.

Her legs moved as if on their own accord, and she got up from the chair. A surge of nausea engulfed her, and she stumbled into the wall.

Dr. Kahn rushed from his chair. "Ms. Black, are you okay?"

Maggie steadied herself against the wall. Her careful composure crumbling away. She would never be okay again. Never get back what she lost. Her ears rang, and the contents of her stomach churned dangerously.

"Please, sit down."

Maggie let the doctor lead her back to the chair. She didn't resist. Couldn't resist. Her mind was everywhere and nowhere at once. Her chest tightened and her vision blurred. "I need to be alone," she whispered.

"Are you sure?"

"Go!" Maggie yelled, barely holding on to any semblance of control.

Dr. Kahn nodded and headed for the door. "You can stay in here for as long as you need. I'll be outside."

A guttural cry escaped Maggie's lips as soon as the door closed. Reality stabbed through her chest like a physical pain, cracking, splintering, *shattering* her heart into a thousand unrepairable pieces.

Maggie fell from the chair and doubled over.

She cradled her belly and shuddered at the emptiness. At the hollow feeling growing inside her where her child should be. Tears flooded her eyes, hot and angry and unrelenting until she feared she'd drown right there on the office floor. She didn't care if the world stopped spinning. She didn't care if she never got up again.

Maggie didn't know how long she sat there on the doctor's office floor. At some point, he came in to check on her and left a cup of tea in her hand. It was cold now.

She'd run out of tears, left with shaking hiccups that left her feeling sick and wrung dry.

A buzzing broke the silence in the room. Maggie searched for the sound and traced it to her handbag.

Reaching over, Maggie tipped the contents out until her phone landed on her lap. Her eyes were sore, and she couldn't make out the name of the person calling on the screen.

Was it Leon?

Oh god. What would she tell Leon? She couldn't tell him, couldn't break his heart the way hers was breaking. But she couldn't *not* tell him either. She had to say something.

"Hello?"

"Maggie, I have a new assignment for you. How soon can you get here?"

She closed her eyes. It wasn't Leon. Bishop's voice echoed in her ear, so matter-of-fact, so to-the-point, breaking what little was left of her. The pain was too much. Too real.

"Maggie?"

The concern in Bishop's voice was like a shot of adrenaline. Her training kicked in, her frantic mind building a wall around her heart to protect itself. It shoved down every feeling, every hope, every dream. Her training chipped away at everything that made Maggie a person, carved out every emotion until all that was left was a hollow shell with a singular purpose.

Brick by brick she restored the obliterated pieces of her protective walls and replaced them with impenetrable titanium. Nothing could get through. Nothing could be allowed in.

No one would ever get in again.

"Maggie, are you there?"

Maggie held her phone back to her ear, her voice crystal clear. "I'll be right in."

THE DEFECTOR IS COMING FEBRUARY 2018!

Check out the next installment of the gripping Maggie Black Case Files series.

Paris. A terrorist threat. One chance to save a city.

In the aftermath of a horrific terrorist attack in London, secret agent Maggie Black is sent to Paris to stop the culprits from striking again.

Struggling with grief from a recent personal loss, Maggie's mission is about more than serving her country. She wants revenge against the home-grown terrorists who shook London to its core. With the help of a certain ex-agent turned rogue Scotsman, Maggie must race against time before Paris and its people meet the same fate.

From the glitz and glam of the city's elite social circles, to the rough and ready streets of the outer ghettos, Maggie must track down the terrorists before they ring in the new year with a literal bang. But the clock is ticking, and Maggie must decide if she can trust someone from inside the enemy camp...

Get your copy of The Defector today!

NEVER MISS A RELEASE!

Thank you so much for reading The Witness. I hope you enjoyed it!

I have so much more coming your way. Never miss a release by joining my free VIP club. You'll receive all the latest updates on my upcoming books as well as gain access to exclusive content and giveaways!

To sign up, simply visit https://jackmcsporran.com/vendettasignup.

Thank you for reading THE WITNESS! If you enjoyed the book, I would greatly appreciate it if you could consider adding a review on your bookstore of choice.

Reviews make a huge difference to the success or failure of a book, especially for newer writers like myself. The more reviews a book has, the more people are likely to take a shot on picking it up. The review need only be a line or two, and it really would make the world of difference for me if you could spare the three minutes it takes to leave one.

With all my thanks,

Jack McSporran

KILL ORDER IS OUT NOW!

Check out the first full-length instalment of the gripping
Maggie Black series.

Deadly. Beautiful. On the run.

When secret agent Maggie Black agrees to protect the
Mayor of London, she thinks she's in for a boring night of
babysitting. The simple job gets a lot more complicated
when an assassin arrives and takes out the Mayor, framing
Maggie as the killer.

Unable to explain the evidence against her, Maggie is
branded a traitor and hunted by the very people she once

fought beside. With no one to turn to, Maggie relies on the one person who has always had her back—herself.

From the hidden nightclubs of Madrid, to the dark streets of Moscow, Maggie must delve into the depths of the criminal underworld to unearth the truth, and fast. Because time is running out and the enemy is closer than she thinks...

Get your copy of Kill Order today!

A SNEAK PEEK INSIDE KILL ORDER...

CHAPTER 1

CANNES, FRANCE

18 MAY

Maggie Black scanned the top deck of the luxury yacht and searched for her target.

A sea of people crowded the open space. Everyone from A-list actors and rock stars to wannabes and groupies were all there for the annual Cannes Film Festival. Even the patient onboard staff seemed impressed as they waited on Hollywood royalty.

The security guards were less impressed. Maggie made sure to keep an extra eye on them. They wandered among the guests in suits that strained against muscled arms, their postures rigid and wires barely hidden in their ears. Blending in wasn't on their list of priorities – unlike Maggie's.

"What did you say your name was again?" asked an irritating brunette to Maggie's left. The stench of cigarette smoke and vodka assaulted her with the woman's every breath.

"Eva," Maggie replied, swirling her glass of water on the rocks. She leaned against the rails of the balcony and looked over the woman's shoulder, feigning interest in whatever it was she was saying.

Music blared from a deejay booth in the center of the partial deck as people well past drunk danced under the glow of the moon, its light glittering off the water as the yacht bobbed a half mile out from the port.

"And what do you do?" the brunette asked, who'd introduced herself as Brooke. Or Becky. Or something like that.

"I'm a model." Maggie didn't bother looking at her conversation partner. She was far more interested in the guard nearest her, and the flash of his pistol as he adjusted his jacket. A black Smith and Wesson from the looks of it. Her hand itched for her own 9mm Glock 19, but it was back in her hotel room.

The crew had searched everyone before coming onboard, and her tight-fitting red dress could hardly conceal a weapon like that. Tonight, Maggie was armed with her wit and her fists.

"Funny, I don't recognize you," Brooke said, the hint of a sneer edging at the corner of her ruby lips.

"Most of my work is international. I did a shoot in Japan last week."

The shoot – two bullets in a Japanese businessman. One in his chest and one in the head to make sure. The British government didn't take too kindly to those caught selling malware to their enemies. In this case, a militia group planning a cyber-attack against the National Health Service.

Maggie flipped her waves of long blond hair to the side and turned to gaze over the deck below.

Plush sofas sat in clusters around glass tables, each of them covered with champagne bottles and bowls of suspicious-looking white powder piled high in the center.

She moved from face to face, evaluating then discarding them one by one. None of them matched the image of the reporter she'd memorized.

Then she saw him. Adam Richmond. Investigative reporter, trust fund playboy, and seller of classified information.

Brooke yapped in Maggie's ear about some movie producer she was seeing, but Maggie paid her no mind. She focused all her attention on the tall, dark, handsome man chatting up a beautiful woman near the bar.

The woman touched his arm and laughed at whatever Adam said. Her clear interest seemed to bore Adam, and his gaze moved from the woman to the rest of the party.

Condensation dripped down Maggie's glass as she took a sip. The day's heat lingered into the night, making Maggie's pale skin glow amid the humid air. The sky had bled out and bruised to a dark purple, promising another ideal day for the film festival. Though not everyone onboard would see the sun rise.

Adam's eyes traveled towards the top deck and landed on Maggie. He grinned at her, the woman beside him forgotten. Maggie watched him with open interest and tucked a strand of hair behind her ear.

He gestured to the bar, where a barman placed two glasses of bubbling champagne on the counter. *Smooth.*

Maggie abandoned her spot at the railing, leaving a flustered Brooke behind without a goodbye, and made her way to him. She took her time travelling down the stairs, allowing her leg to peek out from the slit of her dress, feeling his eyes take her in from head to toe.

As she reached the bottom step, Adam dug into his jacket pocket and brought a cellphone to his ear. His face grew serious as he spoke, his attention stolen from her. Maggie frowned. She made for the bar, but a group of partiers interrupted her path and blocked her view of the target.

When they dispersed, Adam was gone.

Maggie picked up her pace and reached the bar. "The man who was just standing here, where did he go?"

The barman shrugged, busy shaking cocktails and hounded with calls for service from the other guests.

Maggie scanned the bar, but Adam was nowhere to be found. *Shit.*

She scoured the whole deck in search for him, heat rising to her cheeks. A drunk man stumbled into her and stood on the bottom of her dress, pinning her to the spot. Maggie yanked the dress back and shoved the guy away from her. If only she could have worn trousers instead of an insufferable dress.

Holding the train away from her feet, she weaved through the party and headed inside, closing the heavy watertight door behind her.

The bass from the speakers outside hummed through the wooden floors, adding to the rocking of the water as Maggie hurried down the corridor. Her sea legs had suffered much worse than the tame waves of the Mediterranean, allowing her to move with ease, even in killer heels.

Passing a lounge area with a grand piano nestled in the corner, she smiled at those standing around it, singing songs and taking shots of amber liquid. *At least someone gets to enjoy the cruise,* she thought as she continued deeper into the heart of the yacht.

Maggie rounded a corner and took a flight of stairs leading down to the sleeping quarters on the deck below. Voices made her freeze.

"No," said a muffled voice. "I don't want to."

"Yes, you do." The second voice was deep. Slurred. "You've been hanging over me all night."

"Please."

"Shh," the male voice cooed. "You know you want it."

Maggie leaned down to get a look.

A man in his fifties had a young girl pinned against the wall, a meaty hand covering her mouth to stop her from calling out or screaming.

Maggie's nails dug into her palm. She continued down

the stairs and marched up behind the man. "Hey," she called, grabbing the man's shoulder.

"We're busy here." His scowl was soon replaced with a sloppy smile. He whistled, looking Maggie up and down. "Want to join in?"

Maggie grimaced at the man, whose shirt was soaked through with sweat. "Get your hands off her."

The man laughed and returned his focus to the frightened girl. "If you're not interested, piss off before I lose my patience."

Maggie took a deep breath. She couldn't afford to cause a scene or waste time. She needed to find Adam.

The man laughed at her and shook his head. "Stupid bitch."

Maggie grabbed him again and spun him around to face her. She smashed her fist into his bulbous nose, the bone cracking with a delicious snapping sound.

Blood flooded from his nostrils and ran down his chin.

"You broke my fucking nose!" The man lunged at her, but Maggie was ready for him. She caught him with a mean right hook, sending him crashing to the floor with a thump.

The girl leaned against the wall and blinked at Maggie. Her eyes were dilated, and black hair stuck to the sides of her face.

"You okay?" Maggie asked.

The girl stared at her knocked-out attacker and gave a little nod.

"Good. Get out of here and don't tell anyone what happened."

"What about him?" she asked.

"I'll deal with it. Now go, and make sure you drink plenty of water until the yacht gets back to the port." Cocaine and alcohol was one cocktail the girl could do without.

"I will. Thanks." The girl backed away then ran upstairs and out of sight.

Maggie rested her hands on her hips and sighed. She kicked the big lump with the tip of her shoe, then hoisted him up by the arms and dragged him into a nearby supply closet. Maggie shut the door and allowed herself a brief moment to catch her breath before moving on. The dead weight of the man, combined with the heat, sent trickles of sweat down her back.

The lower deck was deserted, the hum of the party echoing from above. Maggie walked towards the aft until the music died enough to hear waves sloshing against the sides of the yacht. She reached a wide hallway with numbered rooms running along either side. Someone had left a door ajar, which revealed a large suite with a king-sized bed and a private balcony.

Her reports said Adam Richmond was staying onboard the yacht during his stay in Cannes. One of his many high roller friends owned the vessel, an investment banker on Wall Street. Adam must have a private room. Somewhere.

Maggie strained her ears and listened for any signs of

life. She tried the first door, but it was locked. As was the next.

This is taking too long. Maggie felt around for the light switch. She flicked off the lights and allowed her eyes to settle. There. At the end of the row to the left.

Light emanated in a thin strip from under the bedroom door. She grinned. *Bingo.*

Maggie turned the lights back on and crept toward the door. She pressed her ear against the wood, careful to stay out of view from the peephole. Footsteps. She was sure of it.

Maggie gripped the door handle, hoping it wasn't locked, and turned it. The door swung open and she stumbled inside, pretending to lose her balance.

Adam jumped in his chair, closing his laptop before turning to face her.

"Oh," Maggie said, wobbling on her feet, "this isn't Brooke's room."

"No, it's not." Adam got up from his chair and ushered her towards the door. He stopped when he got up close to her, his face brightening. "You're the woman from the top deck."

"And you're the man from the bar." Maggie let out a laugh. "I'm sorry. I was looking for my friend, and I got the room numbers mixed up."

"A happy coincidence." Adam crossed the room and opened a minibar, taking out a bottle of cognac. "How about that drink?"

Maggie looked back out into the hall. "I should really be getting back."

"Oh, come on. Just one drink. I insist." Adam shot her a wide smile, his schoolboy charm laid on as thick as his upper-class drawl.

Maggie pretended to consider his offer and shrugged. "Well, if you *do* insist." She closed the door behind her with a soft *click*.

She eyed the closed laptop as Adam poured the drinks into curved crystal glasses. Maggie didn't know what secrets lay inside the hard drive or who the reporter planned on selling them to, but she knew one thing. The transaction would never take place. Not on her watch.

Adam returned and handed her a filled glass. He held his own to hers and they clinked their glasses.

"I'm Adam, by the way."

"Eva," Maggie said, biting her lip. She tossed back her glass in one gulp, and the cognac burned down her throat in a comforting warmth.

Adam's eyebrows rose and then he followed suit, smacking his lips.

"The party couldn't hold your attention?" Maggie asked, brushing her hand against his.

"Let's just say things have certainly picked up, thanks to you."

Maggie gave him a playful push. "Charmer."

He grinned at that, and Maggie suppressed the urge to roll her eyes. A light breeze swept in from the balcony, the curtain sweeping up like a phantom warning of things to come.

"I don't mean to be forward," he said, stepping closer so his chest pressed against hers, "but what would happen if I tried to kiss you right now?"

Maggie raised her head and whispered into his ear. "Why don't you try and find out?"

Adam closed his eyes and moved his head towards her with parted lips.

Maggie placed her hands at either side of his face and leaned towards him. Before Adam Richmond's lips could touch her own, she tightened her grip and jerked her hands with a savage twist.

His neck snapped. A clean, precise break.

They always were.

Maggie let go, and Adam collapsed to the floor, his head lolling to the side.

She stepped over him and sat down at the desk, the seat still warm from the reporter's body, which now grew cold on the floor.

She opened the laptop, took out a portable USB stick from her bra, and plugged it into the port at the side.

Taking a quick glance at the folders stored in the hard drive, Maggie transferred the files onto the USB.

Five percent complete. The green bar grew longer as each file downloaded. *Ten percent.*

A loud knock rapped on the door. "Mr. Richmond, are you okay? We heard a crash."

Maggie's heart leapt in her ribcage. The man's phrasing was not lost on her.

We.

Maggie tapped the side of the laptop. "Come on, come on."

Twenty percent complete.

Sliding out of her heels, Maggie slipped off her dress and stripped down to the thermal bathing suit concealed beneath. She leaned down and collected one of her heels.

Fifty percent complete.

Maggie stared at the body. The man behind the door called again. "Mr. Richmond? I'm coming in."

Bollocks.

The door swung open as Maggie charged across the room. She surprised the first guard, swinging her shoe to meet his head. The heel hit his temple, and blood spurted out like oil from a well.

The next guard was ready for her.

She sent a punch to Maggie's gut, forcing the air out her lungs. The woman reached for her gun, but Maggie charged into her side and rammed her against the door. Their impact slammed the door shut and they tripped over the fallen guard, who squirmed around like a fish out of water, holding his head to keep his brain inside.

Maggie scrambled to her feet, but the woman grabbed her hair and sent her reeling back.

She went with the momentum, hissing as hair ripped

out from her scalp. Maggie rolled into the fall and kicked up, her bare heel connecting with the woman's jaw.

The guard collapsed beside her now unconscious partner.

Maggie returned to the laptop, picking up the woman's gun as she went.

Eighty percent complete.

Footsteps sounded outside, coming closer. She counted four different gaits before she sent six rounds through the door.

Ninety-five percent complete.

There was a commotion outside the door, and it barged open, hitting the fallen guards.

Ninety-eight percent complete.

Someone grunted on the other side of the door as they shoved, sliding the fallen guards forward across the floor.

One-hundred percent complete.

Maggie pulled out the USB and scooped up the laptop. Behind her, the guards shoved the door open enough to fit through.

She reached the balcony and launched the laptop overboard. It landed in the water with a satisfying splash and sank to the murky depths below.

A call came from behind her as the first guard slipped through the gap. Maggie aimed and shot the guard through the thigh. He fell to the ground as three more entered the room and more guards shouted in the corridor.

Maggie dropped the gun and turned back to the

balcony. She ran forward and leapt in the air. Her body passed over the railings, and she positioned herself into a dive and met the water as gunshots carried out through the night.

CHAPTER 2

LONDON, GREAT BRITAIN

19 MAY

Maggie turned the keys in the lock and entered her apartment. A pile of letters lay on the floor waiting for her. She bent down with a groan, her muscles aching from the events of the night before, and nudged the door shut with her foot.

Bills, junk mail, bank statements, take out menus. Nothing important. She tossed them onto the kitchen counter with her keys, kicked off her boots, and wheeled her suitcase into her bedroom. She'd unpack later.

The air in the apartment was stale from disuse. Maggie lit a lemon scented candle, sitting it on the table beside the large living room windows. She peered out at the city skyline, the River Thames flowing past The O2 arena, illuminated like the towers behind it, which belonged to Canary Wharf's most influential banks.

Her reflection stared back at her. She looked tired, her

hair pulled back from her face and bags resting under her ice blue eyes.

Maggie turned away, taking off her coat and draping it over her leather corner couch. A red flickering light caught her attention, the answering machine blinking to alert her of a new message.

Just one. She hadn't been home for over two weeks.

Maggie played the message and plodded over to the fridge to appease her grumbling stomach. Empty, aside from a jar of pickles and a container of something that had long since passed its sell by date. Maggie dumped the container in the bin and ran a hand over her head.

The message played and a woman's voice filled the open plan living space.

"Hi, this is Laura from First Class Travel. I'm calling to fill you in on some of our latest deals as you bought a holiday from us eighteen months ago. I guess you're at work right now, so phone me back when you can. Remember, life isn't all work and no play. You deserve some down time, and we have the perfect hot spots for you to choose from. Bye for now."

Maggie deleted the message and stared at the now empty answering machine. It felt like all she did was travel, though never for pleasure. Even the trip Laura the travel agent mentioned went unused; Maggie was stuck undercover in Morocco at the time.

A familiar shadow crossed the floor of her balcony and pressed up to the sliding door.

Maggie let the black cat in, her only visitor to the riverside apartment since she bought the place last year.

"Hello, Willow." Maggie scratched the cat behind the ears.

Willow rubbed herself against Maggie and circled around her legs, purring up at her. For a stray, Willow was a rather affectionate feline.

Maggie rummaged through the cupboards in the kitchen in search of a can of tuna to feed her furry friend, but like the fridge, they were a barren wasteland.

Willow meowed.

"Chinese food it is then."

Maggie called the restaurant around the corner and placed her usual order. Thirty minutes later, her chicken chow mein and spring rolls arrived, along with steamed fish for Willow.

She switched on the TV, but nothing held her attention for long. There was a spy film showing on one of the movie channels, and Maggie laughed at the ridiculous gadgets featured. Give her an old-fashioned gun or knife any day.

Turning off the TV, Maggie finished her meal in peaceful silence. She fell back on her couch, still smelling as new as the day it arrived, and pulled her bare feet up, closing her eyes as Willow snuggled into her.

A few minutes later, Maggie was back on her feet, pacing around her unused home. It was always like that after a mission, especially one that involved wet work.

Unlike her television, Maggie couldn't simply press an off switch. She'd lost count of how many lives she'd taken over the years, her first at the ripe young age of fifteen. Perhaps she didn't want to know the number.

She could ring Ashton, but he would be busy. The man had never seen a Friday night he didn't like; not that he needed the weekend as an excuse to get up to no good. Besides, she hadn't spoken to him for almost a month. Hopping from one job to the next was a sure-fire way to annihilate any resemblance of a social life.

Her thoughts travelled to Leon, but Maggie was fast to shove them aside.

Fed and watered with a belly full of fish, Willow gave herself a shake, leapt off the couch, and left the way she came in, back out into the night and leaving Maggie alone.

It took all of five minutes before Maggie collected her computer from the coffee table and fired it up. She inserted the USB stick from her mission and downloaded the files she copied off Adam Richmond's computer.

Hours passed as Maggie combed over the contents, reading articles the reporter had penned himself, scrolling through emails from his work and personal accounts, and clicking from one image to the next in his photo folder.

It was almost midnight when she came across something that caught her eye, though it wasn't what she had expected to discover.

Maggie grabbed her mobile and rang one of the few

numbers stored in her contacts. The person at the other end answered after three rings.

"We need to meet."

CHAPTER 3
20 MAY

Maggie arrived at Westminster Station by way of Canning Town, maneuvering through the crowds of eager tourists and early risers, and up the stone steps out onto Bridge Street.

Big Ben watched her as she buttoned her jacket and crossed Parliament Street, continuing down Great George Street. A mass of enraged gray clouds hung over her, threatening rain in typical British fashion for the approaching summer.

She stopped into a café for a much-needed coffee and then cut through St. James's Park. Maggie stopped by the bridge and sipped her drink while she watched some children feed the ducks. Boisterous pigeons swooped down and stole the pieces of bread from their little hands with the skill of London's best thieves.

Maggie arrived at her destination soon after, staring up at the five-story office building on King Street that served as the Unit's headquarters. Disguised as Inked

International, a global stationery supplier, the boring nature of the business gave those not in-the-know no reason to walk through the doors.

The only time anyone ever tried to enter was when they stumbled home from The Golden Lion, an old-school pub next door where Maggie spent one too many nights drinking her way through their collection of whiskies in her early years as an agent.

Maggie swiped her security pass at the entrance. The locks clicked open, and Maggie walked to the elevators, her heels clacking on the marble floor. She entered the empty cab, pressed the button for the top floor, and waited.

"Hold on," came a voice before a foot wedged between the closing doors. The man pried them open and stood beside her in the confined space.

Maggie focused on keeping her face expressionless, her heart fluttering at the sight of him. She cleared her throat, the familiar woody scent of his favorite aftershave dancing in her nose.

"Hi, Leon."

"How you doing, Maggie?" he asked in his deep, gravelly voice.

"Just back from an assignment last night. You?"

"Can't complain." Leon hit the button for the fourth floor. "I thought you just came back from Japan the other week?"

"Are you keeping tabs on me?" Maggie craned her

neck to meet his dark brown eyes for the first time. At six foot three, Leon Frost had over half a foot on her.

"I worry, that's all," he said, his white shirt crisp and bright against his black skin. "Every agent needs some downtime after being out there."

"I'm a big girl, I can look after myself."

Leon sighed and rubbed a strong hand over his close-trimmed beard. "I didn't mean it like that."

It was always like that these days. Both with so much to say to each other, yet saying nothing at all.

They stood in awkward silence until the elevator pinged and opened at Leon's floor. He stepped out, and the cab felt empty without him.

Leon stopped and turned back to her. "You look good, Maggie."

"You too," she said, gripping onto her jacket sleeve.

The doors closed between them, and Maggie took a deep, shaking breath. Seeing Leon was never easy, especially when she wasn't prepared for it.

Straightening her back, she swept her feelings to the side as the elevator stopped on her floor. By the time she stepped out, she was back to normal, her training kicking in.

Never let anyone see you sweat.

Brice Bishop was waiting for her in his office with a cup of tea in his hand.

"Maggie," he said, the remnants of a Manchester accent still in his inflection. "Nice to have you back."

162

Maggie sat down across from his desk. "Thanks."

Bishop's office was clean and Spartan, the result of a long career in the military before he joined the Unit. His phone buzzed and he read the message, tossing it back on the desk with a heavy sigh.

"Everything okay?"

"June," said Bishop, needing no further clarification. The divorce with his wife had been a long and messy one, their relationship barely civil and only so because of their kids.

"What now?"

"I finally get the girls next weekend, and she's trying to cancel."

"Why?"

"She and *Brian*," he said, the distain for his ex-wife's new fiancé clear from the way he growled the man's name, "decided to take a family holiday that week. If I cancel, I don't get to see them for at least another three weeks."

"And if you don't, you're the bad one for cancelling their holiday," Maggie finished. It had taken a while for Bishop to get back on good terms with his teenage daughters, both girls siding with their mother during the divorce.

Bishop leaned back in his chair. "June's design, of course. She should have been an agent."

"I'm sorry, Bishop."

Bishop tried to shrug like it was nothing, but he didn't quite pull it off.

For a man in his late fifties, he still clung to his brown

hair which he kept cropped at the sides like he was still a soldier. Crow's feet perched at the corners of his eyes, his skin tough as leather, and nose bent out of shape from when Maggie had broken it during her first official mission.

To the untrained eye, Bishop appeared as just another businessman living in London who looked after himself and wore expensive suits. It was all deliberate, of course. Brice Bishop was so much more than that, and stories of his days as an agent still passed around the Unit like folktales. He was one of the best.

"Enough about that. I trust everything went well?"

Maggie nodded. "All according to plan."

"Excellent."

"There was one thing."

"Oh?"

"I couldn't find any of the stolen secrets on Richmond's laptop." Not one file. She searched for hidden folders and encrypted documents disguised as something else, but the laptop was empty.

"You read the computer files?"

"I figured I should check what the secrets were, in case any of them were an imminent threat to national security." And out of sheer curiosity to find out what was so classified that Richmond had to die, but Maggie kept that to herself.

Bishop nodded. "Good thinking."

Maggie leaned forward in her chair. "But that's just it. I didn't find any."

"Nothing?" Bishop frowned.

"Not nothing, but not what we were looking for."

Maggie got up and turned on the computer. It was linked to a projector Bishop used when hosting meetings. Like she did at her apartment, she plugged in the USB stick and selected some of the files of note.

"I trolled through every file on here. Junk for the most part, but one folder in particular stood out." Maggie clicked the first file and it appeared on the projector screen on the wall. "Richmond was working on a story, investigating a private and commercial property developer named Brightside Property and Construction Limited."

Bishop clasped his hands. "What was his angle?"

"Corruption. Apparently, the company applied for planning permission on a plot of land in the East End, but it was declined." Richmond had acquired a copy of the application to prove it.

"Why?"

Maggie brought up an article that had made it onto the BBC News website. "The land is home to a row of government assisted houses owned by the local council. The residents are refusing to move."

"Where does the corruption come in?" Bishop asked, his tea growing cold on the desk.

"Brightside recently purchased the houses from the government, which now makes the homes private rentals.

Brightside increased the rent payments to unaffordable levels to push the residents out."

Bishop shook his head. "Legally evicting them. Sly bastards."

"It's worked for the most part," Maggie continued, "but a few of the residents are causing a stink about it and going to the press. There have been reports of intimidation, too. Residents claim men knocked on their doors in the middle of the night and threatened them, warning them to move."

Richmond had gathered some written testimonies and a few names, but nothing concrete. It didn't take long for Maggie to find a way into the Metropolitan Police's records and hunt down police reports to corroborate the stories.

"I did some digging. Similar reports have been made against Brightside in other developments in London and surrounding areas over the years."

Maggie clicked on another file. A photo of a body appeared on the screen, an old man beaten to death, his face purple and swollen.

"Eric Solomon was found dead in his home, the victim of a supposed break-in."

Bishop examined the photos on the screen. "What makes you think he wasn't?"

"The week before his body was found, Mr. Solomon turned down a substantial financial offer from Brightside to move. He'd purchased the council house he was living in before Brightside took over and procured the surrounding land. His refusal to move would have stopped their plans to knock down the houses and build a shopping center on the land."

Maggie brought up the proposed plans for the construction. Richmond had really done his homework.

"With the old man dead, Brightside could carry on with their plans," Bishop said, tying up all the pieces with a neat bow.

"That's what I'm thinking." Maggie pulled the USB from the computer. "Though it seems strange for someone like Adam Richmond to investigate all this while preparing to sell classified documents to the highest bidder."

"Perhaps it was part of his cover," ventured Bishop. "He was an investigative reporter after all."

Bishop could be right. Maggie sat back down and slid the USB across the desk to him. "I don't know all the big players yet, but I will soon enough. I'm pretty sure Richmond was on to something here. Something big."

"Great work. Really." Bishop leaned back in his chair. "I'll speak with the Director General and see if she can dig anything up from the guys at MI5. They might already be looking into the dealings of this company." He shook his head. "Richmond must have kept the stolen files somewhere else."

"I can contact Ms. Helmsley if you want," Maggie offered. The Director General was known as a pit bull in a power suit around the Unit, but Maggie liked her. She had a knack for seeing through bullshit and kept the men running around for her like they were little boys and she their headmistress.

"No, that's all right, I'll do it." Bishop slid a manila folder in front of her. "I have a favor to ask of you in the meantime."

"What?" Maggie eyed the folder but didn't pick it up.

"The Mayor of London is the keynote speaker at an international business conference in the financial district and has requested a chaperone."

Maggie sighed. "When?"

"Tonight," said Bishop. "Nina will be there, too, following the same orders for the Foreign Secretary."

"Why can't another agent do it?" The last thing Maggie wanted to do was go back out on a mission. She'd only just gotten home. "I saw Leon coming in."

"Leon is already assigned to another case. All my other agents are tied up."

Maggie remained quiet. If she wanted a career in babysitting, she would've been a nursery teacher.

"It's only for a couple of hours," added Bishop, giving her that pleading look she hated.

Maggie drooped her shoulders. "I can look after them both on my own. No need to send two agents for this type of job." If she wasn't getting the night off, at least Nina could.

"Nina is going, too. You really need to learn to work

with others," Bishop said, not for the first time. "You can't do everything on your own."

Maggie folded her arms. It wasn't that she didn't like Nina. They had known each other since they joined the Unit at sixteen. She just worked better alone. "Fine, but I'm taking my annual leave after this."

"Of course." Bishop handed her the file containing what she would need to know for the evening's event. "Thanks, Maggie."

Maggie took the manila folder and left Bishop's office. Maybe she would call that travel agent back after all.

CHAPTER 4

The taxi took a left from Leadenhall Street and turned into St Mary Axe, where a swanky new hotel had opened on the corner of Bevis Marks, right next to The Gherkin.

Maggie paid the fare and stepped out into the cold. The sky's earlier promise of rain came through, and huge droplets plummeted down from the heavens.

She ducked under the covered entrance to the Baltic Hotel and shook her umbrella out.

"I'll take that for you, Madam," said a man by the door, ushering her inside.

"Thank you," she said. "I'm here for the conference."

The man pointed across the room to where a sign stood for the event. "Straight ahead."

Maggie walked through the foyer and arrived at a large and glamorous conference room, decked out with chandeliers hanging from the high ceilings that overlooked round tables. At the back of the conference room, Maggie noted the podium where the mayor would give his talk.

The tables were set with fine porcelain dishes, crystal glassware, and golden cutlery. The staff had even arranged the napkins into elegant swans. Ten seats a piece were tucked under the tables, upholstered in fine gold suede to match the intricate filigree design of the wallpaper.

Along the bar sat buckets of champagne resting on ice, ready for when the attendees arrived.

The organizers had spared no expense, appropriate given the high-profile guests could bring millions of pounds in foreign investments into London's private sector.

Nina stood waiting for her near the bar as staff milled around the room making final touches to the pristine layout.

"I've scoped out the place," announced Nina by way of hello. "Everything's in order."

She wore a sleek gown with a plunging neckline, the emerald fabric bringing out the green in her hazel eyes. It also did a good job of hiding the knives Maggie knew would be strapped to Nina's thighs. She had a fondness for getting up close and personal with her enemies.

"Good," replied Maggie, taking a quick look around. "Where are our charges?"

"Upstairs in one of the suites," Nina said as she headed out to the foyer and climbed the stairs.

Maggie followed, cursing the dress code. Why did she always find herself stuck in a dress? At least the black number she wore tonight wasn't hugging her hips. Her gun sat in its holster around her thigh, the familiar weight like a deadly comfort blanket.

"Here's your ear piece." Nina handed it over to Maggie along with a clipboard, both playing the role of event coordinators for their cover.

"It's already wired in to the right frequency." Nina spoke into the little microphone of her own device. "Testing."

"One, two, three," Maggie replied, securing hers around her ear, careful not to disturb her chignon hairdo. If she had to wear a dress, the least her hair could do was to stay out of her face.

"How was Cannes?" Nina asked, slowing down to walk by Maggie's side.

They were around the same height, but where Maggie was curved with vulpine features, Nina was lithe and all sharp angles, from her cutting cheekbones to her pointed nose.

"A pain in the neck," Maggie said. "The weather was nice though."

Nina shook her head. "Bishop really needs to stop sending me to places that require thermals."

"That's what you get for speaking Russian."

Nina huffed, a playful grin edging her lips. "You speak it, too, and you got to party on a yacht."

Maggie held up her hands. "Hey, I'm not complaining."

"Must be nice being the favorite," Nina teased, nudging her.

While preferring to work alone, if Maggie had to work with anyone, she was glad it was Nina. They were both teenagers when Bishop recruited them. Though they viewed each other as rivals at first, it didn't take long for them to become good friends. There weren't many women in the Unit, so they bonded quickly.

Like most old boys' clubs, the Unit had some work to do to bridge the gender imbalance. One too many meetings suffered from an overload of alpha-male testosterone. Not that Maggie or Nina had any trouble being heard. They just had to trample on a few toes first.

When they reached the third floor, Nina led Maggie to the corner suite, walking past two armed men who stood sentry before the entrance. Nina stopped in front of the door. "Fair warning, the Foreign Secretary is rather sloshed."

"Some boys just can't handle their drink," Maggie said with a sigh.

Nina ran a hand through her locks of straight chestnut hair and gave Maggie a wink.

The suite was as expected, given how the rest of the Baltic Hotel was decorated. The designers were fans of gold and rich creams, the primary colors of the sitting area that separated the bedrooms and bathroom. White lilies bloomed in several vases around the space and filled the air with their light floral scent.

A man got up from the couch on unstable legs. Nina was right, George Moulton was drunk, and from the triple measure in his hand, he had no intentions of stopping.

"Very nice indeed," he said, his voice loud and irritating. He studied them with glassy eyes, his fake tan a shade too orange to fool anyone into thinking it was real. "Why does Bishop only recruit sexy girls?"

Maggie responded with a raised eyebrow, biting her tongue to refrain from assassinating him with a response. At least she wasn't in charge of babysitting him for the night.

Nina stiffed at the mention of Bishop. "Is anyone else here?" she hissed.

"Relax, it's just us," said Moulton, shaking his head.

Nina glared at him.

Knowledge of the Unit was strictly classified due its propensity to cross the line of what was legal. Only those with a high enough clearance were made aware of its existence. Most of those working for the Secret Intelligence Service weren't even privy to their clandestine faction.

Ignoring the Foreign Secretary, Maggie walked over to the other man in the room. The Mayor of London was busy reading over notecards by the window. "Nice to meet you Mr. Worthington," she said and offered her hand. "I'm Maggie Black."

"A pleasure, and please, call me James," he said, his shake nice and firm. "Thank you for doing this on such short notice. I'm afraid our little event resulted in some anonymous threats, and Brice felt some extra security was in order."

"He doesn't like to take any chances," replied Maggie, cursing Bishop. She could be curled up on her couch in her pajamas, reading a good book with a nice glass of wine right about now.

George Moulton cackled behind them, Nina giggling a polite yet strained laugh along with him. James scowled at the man's back and offered Maggie an apologetic shrug.

"Ready for your speech?" Maggie asked.

"As I'll ever be." James released a heavy exhale. "I'm not good with these things."

James Worthington was new in his role as mayor. His predecessor Edgar Johnston died at the beginning of the year.

The new mayor was a handsome man, in a stiff upper lip sort of way. Not a hair was out of place on his head, his face clean shaven. He wore a smart suit, yet nothing too flashy like the Armani suit Moulton had squeezed into.

Moulton continued spluttering behind them, cracking jokes and lighting a cigar. Maggie had heard better one liners from Christmas crackers. The tendrils of smoke from his cigar circled around the room, drowning out the fresh lilies.

Maggie lowered her voice. "I'm sure you'll do better than him."

That won her a smile. "Yes, well, there's that at least."

"I'm going to take Mr. Moulton down to his table," called Nina. Moulton wasn't due to talk until after the dinner. Hopefully by then he would have the ability to stand, never mind give a speech on UK business.

"See you down there." Maggie turned back to the mayor when the door closed behind Nina. "We've made a sweep of the hotel and surrounding areas and cleared the conference room itself. You're good to go."

"Excellent." James held out his arm. "Shall we?"

Maggie indulged him and linked her arm in his. "It's a nice hotel," she said as they walked downstairs, the armed men following close behind. Voices travelled up from the foyer as the guests arrived in time for the mayor's speech. And the free booze and food.

"Yes, named after the Baltic Exchange. Terrible business."

Maggie was too young to remember the bombing of the building, right on the very street they were in now, but

Bishop had worked on the case. Three people had died that day, and another ninety-one injured.

"The drunken idiot is seated and behaving himself," came Nina's voice in Maggie's ear. "No signs of trouble."

The podium was to the back of the conference room and had its own entrance. The mayor stood behind the curtain, going over his notes one last time before going out.

The real event coordinator was behind the podium, too, ordering helpers around, her cheeks flush and movements flustered.

Maggie watched everyone who came and went, taking in faces and checking all access points.

"All clear here," Maggie said into her microphone just as a man caught her eye.

He strode backstage, but not in an organized rush like the others around him. He moved with a purpose, and that purpose became clear as he approached and reached into his jacket.

Maggie was about to shout when the man lunged at the mayor.

The man pulled out his gun and aimed at his target. Maggie dived in front of the mayor, blocking the man's path. His finger inched toward the trigger, but Maggie got to him first, thrusting his arm into the air. The gun went off and shot into the ceiling, flecks of plaster falling around them like snow.

Screams erupted from the other side of the curtain as guests heard the shot echoing off the walls of the large room. Chairs scraped on the floor and footsteps stampeded as people spilled out of the conference room and into the foyer.

The man was fast, and before the mayor's two personal guards could move three paces, he shot bullets into each of their heads. They crumbled to the floor like lifeless dolls, blood already seeping out of the bullet holes.

Maggie jabbed at the assailant, but he blocked her punch, sending a ringing pain through her arm. He pointed his gun at the mayor once again, but Maggie timed a perfect roundhouse that sent the weapon flying from his grasp.

The gun landed out of sight and Maggie squared up to the assassin, making sure to stay between him and James. If he wanted to reach the mayor, he would need to go through her.

The assassin swung a fist at her, and Maggie ducked back avoiding impact. She reached for her own gun, concealed around her thigh, but the man was on her again, this time catching her in the jaw with a right hook.

Maggie's head snapped to the side, the metallic tang of blood filling her mouth.

With a yell, she bounded forward and kneed him in the stomach, doubling him over. When he straightened back up, he had a knife in his hand, the silver glinting under the light.

The mayor stepped toward her, but Maggie shoved him back out of the way.

The assassin took advantage of her distraction and sliced at her. Maggie noticed the knife at the last second and flinched back, the blade catching on the fabric of her dress. She grabbed his wrist and thrust her palm into the man's elbow, aiming for a break. The bone didn't snap, but the assassin yelped and dropped his weapon.

But the loss of his weapon didn't slow him down. The man spun and rammed into her with his shoulder, forcing Maggie back. He swept his foot across the floor and swiped his leg into hers, sending her careening to the floor in a graceless fall.

He made for the mayor, but Maggie scrambled to her feet and grabbed him by the back of his collar, using his momentum as he stumbled back to trip him up. He fell on the arm she damaged and hissed.

Maggie seized the moment and threw all her weight into a brutal kick to his abdomen. The man groaned a curse and rolled away, holding his stomach as he bounced back up on agile feet. Maggie made for him again, but he turned and ran, heading back the way he came.

"Stay here. Don't come out until I come back for you," she ordered the mayor. "Got it?"

James nodded, wide eyed and panting, leaning against the wall to keep him steady.

Certain he was okay and had heard her, Maggie abandoned her heels, leaped over the dead bodies of the guards, and sped off after the assassin.

The foyer was pandemonium, people pushing and shoving each other out of the way to race from the hotel, all pretense of civility gone. An old man lay on the floor covering his head as others trampled over him to get to safety.

Nina spoke in Maggie's ear. "Maggie what the hell is going on? I heard gun shots."

"Someone tried to take out the mayor," she replied. "I'm in pursuit."

"Where are you? Do you need my help?"

"No. Get the Foreign Secretary out of here. He could be a target, too."

"Copy that," Nina said, her voice cutting in and out. "Go catch the prick."

The alarm interfered with the wire's signal, and it screeched in Maggie's ear. She took it out and tossed it, continuing her chase.

Maggie fought her way through the crowd, eyes set on finding the one responsible for the chaos. Black hair, light brown skin, an unassuming face that blended in well. Spanish from the way he cursed, though she could be mistaken on that. Spanish wasn't on her list of fluent languages.

The alarms wailed through the hotel. New and louder

screams followed, the sirens only panicking the people more.

Event Security tried to settle everyone down and restore order, but it wasn't working. The flight instinct in the guests was well and truly in effect. But not for Maggie. She was in full fight mode.

Maggie spotted Nina across the foyer in a splash of emerald among the crowd, heading out the front door with George Moulton. They met each other's eyes, and Maggie nodded for her to go on. George could be in danger.

Maneuvering her way through the panicked people, Maggie scanned every inch of the room.

There.

The assassin had made it through the crowd and was running up the stairs Maggie had taken with the mayor. The man looked over his shoulder and spotted her moving his way.

Maggie ran, feet cold on the marble floor, and fought her way through the guests. She reached the stairs and took them three at a time, releasing her gun from its holster and gripping it with a firm hold.

She turned the safety off and made it to the second floor.

A door to her left was closing, but no one had come racing out to head downstairs. Maggie caught it before it clicked shut and ducked inside, weapon at the ready.

The tail of a black jacket flashed down the hall as someone turned the corner at a run.

Maggie sprinted after them, her heart pounding and hair slipping out from behind her head. She rounded the corner and laid eyes on her target. Aiming with both hands, Maggie kept running and shot at the assassin.

The bullets missed his head by inches, embedding into the wall. He made a right down another hall of the hotel floor, and Maggie heard a crash.

Sprinting after him, she spotted the busted door to one of the rooms, the wood split off the frame. Gun at the ready, Maggie stepped inside. Something cold brushed against her bare foot, and she stole a glance down. A card. She bent to collect it, keeping her weapon pointed into the darkness of the room. It was a room key, but not for that one, or any other on the second floor. It was for the level above.

"I know you're in here," Maggie said, stepping inside.

Glass shattered further in, and she stormed through, ready to attack.

The assassin was at the window, the cold air blowing in through the broken pane. He took one last look at her before Maggie pulled the trigger.

The man jumped from the window and fell out of sight.

Maggie moved to the window and looked down. He wasn't there.

"Shit."

Things were still up in the air when she returned to the foyer, red faced and kicking herself at failing to apprehend the assassin.

She went to the back of the podium to return to the mayor and report what happened. So much for an easy couple of hours.

Maggie walked in to find the place deserted other than the two bodies lying in a heap on the ground.

She froze.

Not two bodies. Three.

James Worthington, Mayor of London and her charge, was dead.

 et your copy of Kill Order today!

Printed in Great Britain
by Amazon